Escaping Neverland

ISBN 13: 978-1-4621-2352-0

Published by Sweetwater Books, an imprint of Cedar Fort, Inc.
2373 W. 700 S., Springville, UT 84663
Distributed by Cedar Fort, Inc., www.cedarfort.com

LIBRARY OF CONGRESS CATALOGING-IN-PUBLICATION DATA

Names: Lemon, Melissa, 1980- author. | Adaptation of (work): Barrie, J. M.
    (James Matthew), 1860-1937. Peter Pan.
Title: Escaping Neverland / Melissa Lemon.
Description: Springville, Utah : Sweetwater Books, an imprint of Cedar Fort,
    Inc., [2019]
Identifiers: LCCN 2018058280 (print) | LCCN 2019004004 (ebook) | ISBN
    9781462129836 (epub, pdf, mobi) | ISBN 9781462123520 (perfect bound : alk.
    paper)
Subjects: LCSH: Peter Pan (Fictitious character)--Fiction. | Never-Never Land
    (Imaginary place)--Fiction. | LCGFT: Fantasy fiction. | Novels.
Classification: LCC PS3612.E473 (ebook) | LCC PS3612.E473 E83 2019 (print) |
    DDC 813/.6--dc23
LC record available at https://lccn.loc.gov/2018058280

Cover design by Jeff Harvey   NOV 1 2 2019
Cover design © 2019 Cedar Fort, Inc.
Edited by Jessilyn Peaslee and Misty Moncur
Typeset by Kaitlin Barwick

Printed in the United States of America

10 9 8 7 6 5 4 3 2 1

Printed on acid-free paper

For Emery, Regen & Cadence

And for my nieces and nephews:
Krecia, Konner, Cierra L., Taylor, Kaydon, Tara, Kylie,
Cierra E., Justin, Dallin, Brieanne, Dylan, Kobe, Abbie,
William, Josie, Emma, Faith, Dima, Scott, Brooklyn,
Rahel, Ian, Maddie, Keira, Alex, Peter & Brock

Growing up is nothing to fear.

PIRATE TORTURE

Sven's hot breath pulsed in sporadic rhythms across Peter's ear and neck. The pungent stench of fish and garlic wafted into his nostrils, penetrating so deeply Peter thought it would never leave him again. He gagged, his empty stomach threatening to spew up a pool of acid. The pitch blackness surrounding him made his other senses more acute, more capable somehow, and Peter was not glad of the effect it was having on him. He imagined Sven's slim figure, his stringy blond hair tethered in grease, his crooked, yellow teeth. Not all Neverland pirates looked so much like . . . well, pirates. But Sven did, perhaps minus the parrot, patch, and hook. Peter mused over what it would be like to slice off a pirate hand or gouge out one of Sven's eyes. Maybe both. He deserved no less.

Peter's legs and arms shook as he hung in a V shape from ropes tied to his ankles and wrists. The coarse, abrasive hairs of the Never reed ropes constantly cut into his skin, deepening his wounds. It was too dark in Black Cavern to see what exactly the ropes were attached to. Peter guessed Sven had drilled huge screws into the ancient rock ceiling of this hole in the mountain.

Gnashing his teeth and spitting, Sven continued his diatribe. "How many times do you think I'm going to ask? Where is it?" Sven grabbed Peter's shirt and used it to yank Peter even closer, forcing their heads to touch.

With more facetiousness and hot anger than sarcasm, Peter answered. "Was that first question rhetorical, Sven? You know I don't like being asked multiple questions at a time."

"Still bent on playing games, are we? Can you handle that question?"

"I could have, until you asked one on top of it." Sven was such a moron.

A heavy blow came unexpectedly then, straight across Peter's mouth. He jerked, causing a fresh onslaught of rope burn on all four limbs to accompany the pain vibrating through his lips and jaw. "What is wrong with you?" Peter yelled.

"You know what's wrong with me." Sven sounded playful now. Peter wished he would pick a mood. "I was abandoned as a child, had a poor, abhorrent childhood, and turned into a mean, disgusting pirate. There are no secrets between us, Peter, except for the one you keep to yourself now."

"What do you want with it?" Peter's chest flared with fresh anger. Sven had never been quite this abusive before.

"I want to know how old you are."

Peter contemplated this statement. Sven had never even asked before. "Why?"

"Too many questions. I'm in charge here!" The playfulness vanished, replaced with fury.

Forcing a series of deep breaths, Peter tried to calm down. Decades of studying Never fairies had taught him that the one in control was the one who could choose his emotions. Peter allowed the anger to seep from his heart, the curiosity to spill from his brain, and the fear to retreat from his soul. He would not let Sven have any power over him unless it was forcibly and physically taken, as was the case with the ropes. Sven could not tell Peter how to think or feel, or force him to answer any questions.

"Last chance," Sven said in a singsong voice.

Peter wanted to say, "Or what?" but decided against it, not wanting another punch to the face or anywhere else.

"Choosing silence, are we?"

I am, Peter thought. Sven was obviously not done talking. Probably never would be.

Sven turned toward the cavern's opening and shouted, "Send him down!"

What sounded next sent a jolt of panic across Peter's chest. He'd recognize the sound of that gait anywhere. Charlie was so young; his footsteps could almost still be considered a toddler's pitter-patter—the unmistakable slapping of tiny bare feet across the rock floor. Peter flailed, desperately attempting to free himself to no avail.

"Peter, I've come to save you!" The irony of that sentence pierced Peter's consciousness. Nobody had ever come to save Peter. Not really. Peter always did the saving. At least, that's what it felt like. And how was he going to save Charlie now, with his hands and legs bound?

"What are you up to, Sven?" Peter demanded.

"It's too dark for you to see the improvements I've made to Black Cavern," Sven said.

Peter's blood ran cold. Sven's improvements were never good. One of his worst offenses was putting sharp, metal spikes along his ship's plank (try swimming with bleeding feet). He'd also created a serum that attracted Never fairies, capturing them in its stickiness where they died of starvation in the fairy color of deep despair—a plum so dark it was almost black. Of all the captains since Hook, Sven won the prize for being the most vindictive and sadistic pirate. If Sven had made improvements here and had brought little Charlie to try them out, Peter had to do something.

"Let him go, Sven. Then I'll talk."

"No! Talk first." Again, with the hot breath and spitting.

Peter weighed his next decision, wondering how far Sven would go to get what he wanted. "No," he said. "Let him go first. Then I'll talk."

"Tighten the ropes!" Sven spat.

Next thing he knew, Peter's body hoisted even farther off the ground, the ropes pulling and scratching as they worked to straighten his limbs and bring him closer to the ceiling. A jolt of pain surged through his back and limbs. He couldn't tell if the sensation of needle pricks all over his wrists came from the burly, biting ropes or the lack of circulation. Were his hands and feet waking up again? Would he lose blood supply altogether and need an amputation or two? Perhaps he'd be the one needing a hook hand soon.

As the sharp pains settled into a pulsing burn, Peter noticed that the ropes continued to pull, stretching his arms and legs even more. Instead of worrying about the potential for bodily damage, Peter tried to distract himself with other thoughts. How many feet must he be off the rocky floor? With barely any light to see, Peter had no clue, but he thought he could sense the ceiling only just above him. He fought through the numbness to wiggle a finger, trying to see if he could touch the rock.

"What are you doing to him?" Charlie called, beginning to cry.

"Shut up!" Sven said.

Peter tried not to focus on Charlie's small voice or the sound of his cries, or the cruelty of the pirates that must have been holding him. Instead he thought of London. What Peter wouldn't give to leave this place forever and live permanently on planet Earth. He envisioned Westminster Abby, Buckingham Palace, the Thames slothfully winding and jogging through the city.

"I'll only ask once more, Peter. After that, the boy dies."

It seemed an eternity since the pirates had killed one of the Lost Boys. So long that Peter had to dig for the memory. The image of Neverland's lonely graveyard came to mind, situated at the top of a wide hill with only a handful of marked graves. Knowing a killing wasn't impossible, he had no choice now. Peter sighed, his only outer display of the utter defeat consuming him. How had their rivalry come to this? How had things gotten so messed up? "My age calculator is with the mermaids."

Sven began making a ticking sound with his tongue, his marked way of shaming someone when he didn't approve. His tone dripped with mockery, however, and Peter knew Sven only pretended to chide. "Peter, we can't visit the mermaids unless we kill one of them to escape their clutches. You know that. Since you're not a fan of killing the creatures, I presume you left it with them so it wasn't a temptation for you anymore. Don't worry, though. The older we get, the easier it is to obsess over our age. Believe me, I understand completely your wanting to forget how old you are." Turning back toward the other pirates, he added, "Isn't that right, gentlemen?"

They grunted and chuckled with enthusiasm.

"I wouldn't know," Peter said. "I haven't aged in a long time, probably decades." His words had come out sounding forcibly innocent, and Peter winced when he realized as much. He had only been making a frantic attempt to convince the pirate that he hadn't been leaving Neverland on a regular basis, aging each time he did so.

Peter listened to Sven's angry footsteps cross the floor followed by a short struggle presumably with another pirate. Without warning Peter was falling fast. The ropes had been let go. He barely had time to flail his arms and legs before his head and back slammed onto the rock below. Stunned, Peter thought of nothing as Sven ranted about how much he hated lies and such. Peter tried to remember what the mermaids had told him but found it difficult to think. A sharp pain seared through the back of his head and temples, not to mention his shoulders and tailbone, or even his wrists and ankles, which burned like hot ashes just after the last flame blew out. A trickle of wet blood crept from underneath his head.

"We'll keep it safe," the mermaids had told him in their own language. "Nobody will ever find it. But you may come for it whenever you're ready to have it again." Sven was right. Peter had been obsessing about the fact that he was nearing the age of a man. He knew what that meant. But he wasn't ready to leave Neverland yet, and he had no intention of becoming a pirate. Nobody knew about the treaty he'd made with the mermaids to get them to take it. If he allowed Sven to go and demand it, requiring one of their lives, he'd be at their mercy. He had to get it himself. Peter was the only one they would give it to without a fight. Still, Sven didn't need to know this.

"Of course, I've never minded killing a mermaid or two. Perhaps I'll go find it myself," Sven said.

"I'll go and get it for you," Peter whispered. Once he started talking, his lungs decided they were experiencing more pain than any other part of his body. Peter thought of emotions as colors. After being in Neverland so long, he couldn't help it. He pictured a lavender fairy, the color of helplessness. He remembered the first time he'd seen a lavender fairy, its wings caught in the tiny net the Lost Boys used on occasion to catch butterflies for their collection. She had turned this color only when her wings had stopped fluttering, as if she couldn't try another moment. He'd never experienced the emotion before, having always believed that he had options. Neverland had changed so much. Or perhaps only Peter had changed. Sealing his eyes shut, Peter reminisced about letting that fairy go and seeing it turn tan for disorientation, followed right away by royal blue, the color for gratitude.

Gratitude. Again, Peter thought of how nobody ever came to save him. Royal blue was a color, and gratitude an emotion, he would never know. He would go to the mermaids, ask for the dial, and bring it to Sven. With Charlie being threatened, Peter didn't know what else he could do.

Things began to fade, all those acute senses. The faint sound of footsteps echoed in his ears, followed by a brushing across his upper arm as someone lifted his sleeve, and then a searing brand pressed into his shoulder.

Peter yelled, the pain forcing out all other thoughts, except the worry for Charlie. Peter began to lose focus, and Charlie's cries diminished.

A harsh whisper followed. "You'll be one of us soon enough. Mark my words."

Peter guessed that turning him into a pirate was probably Sven's goal. He wondered what would happen if he resisted. Would he end up in the Never graveyard? He'd rather be buried in London. Realizing this, Peter began formulating a plan.

Sven ordered another pirate to cut Peter loose. Charlie ran to Peter's side, then all sounds became distant. The blackness blocking his sight seeped into the crevices of his mind, and everything—light, awareness, knowing—vanished.

ALLIANCE GONE AWRY

*P*eter stared at Brim Lake, knowing the mermaids probably watched him from underneath the rippling water. Dusk permeated the Neverland atmosphere, giving Peter the sense that everything teetered on this moment, just as Autumn Quarter teetered endlessly between light and dark. A shiver ran up his spine. He searched the perimeter of the lake, checking for lurking pirates. Leaves rustled behind him, and Peter jerked around to find Karl.

Peter tried to disguise his surprise but failed. "Karl! What are you doing here?" he asked.

"What is it, Peter? Are you planning to attack the pirates? Are you meeting someone here?"

"Shhhhh," Peter whispered, holding a finger to his lips while he urged the Lost Boy to be quiet. "I'm here to see the mermaids."

"What for?" Karl asked, failing to lower his voice.

"Shhhhh," Peter said. "Go back to the Hollow Tree Wood. I'll be along soon."

"But they'll kill you," Karl whispered.

Peter stared at the boy's silhouette. "I'll be fine," he said. "Promise. Have I ever broken a promise?"

"No, Peter, but—"

"Then go. Look after the others, especially Charlie." Peter remembered how the youngest Lost Boy continued to have nightmares after he'd come to find Peter in Black Cavern. "The pirates are still on Neverland."

Karl's face hardened, his lips in a stern line. "Whatever you say, Peter."

Karl backed away until he turned and disappeared into the thick forest surrounding the lake. A breath escaped Peter's lips, and he raised his head to the Never sky in search of a star to wish on. Yellow and pink light rimmed the horizon, reflecting on the outer edges of the lake.

A round shape emerged from the water and came toward Peter—an eerie sight accompanied by the ominous sound of disturbed water. Long hair floated around the mermaid's scaly skin. Glaring eyes accompanied a human-like face. Never mermaids resembled humans in some ways from the waist up. They had two arms, but their hands lacked fingers. Scales came all the way up to the cheek bones, and they couldn't be described as beautiful, not with their ever-present death stare and fish-like features. Peter couldn't quite make out the color of this mermaid in the twilight, but he thought it might be the same color as a goldfish. The mermaids didn't have names, or leaders. He dealt with whichever creature came to the surface. Never mermaids acted in perfect unison, which was fine so long as they weren't trying to attack Peter.

"Peetah Pahn," the mermaid said once her entire head breached the dark liquid. "*Ha sem fey na wey?*" (Why have you come?)

"*Wey ba na si. Tic fel men wi.*" (I've come to greet you. And retrieve the device.)

The creature's head sunk back below the surface, and Peter took the opportunity to check again for pirates. He bit his bottom lip and drummed his fingers against his blue jeans. He glanced at his dim reflection on the water's surface. It still surprised him how old he looked. His reflection had revealed a boy for so long that Peter still hadn't gotten used to the masculine face staring back at him. Peter stood a little taller, summoning the confidence he needed to deal with a species as treacherous as Never mermaids.

The orangish mermaid reappeared along with two others—one the same color as the water, and the other a bright yellow-green—and they all glared at Peter. None of them spoke, but the one in the center lifted a scaly arm and held out Peter's age calculator in her palm. The appendage resembled a fin but worked much like a human hand.

A sudden splash alerted Peter to the presence of several more mermaids. Peter resisted taking a step back. The new arrivals made a semicircle around the three creatures nearest Peter. While one held the device, the remaining mermaids each lifted a spear and pointed it toward Peter.

He refused to tremble. They'd promised an alliance, or maybe truce was a better word. Still, he knew their finicky nature and prepared for a confrontation.

"*Se mon ky. Ha sem mey na key?*" (Here it is. Why do you want it?)

Peter knew he had to speak quickly, otherwise they'd suspect him of scheming or being dishonest and possibly attack.

"*Wey fel na.*" (I need it.) Peter remained calm but struggled for words. "*Se tu fa lee mi.*" (For protection.)

The mermaids turned to one another and whispered. Peter couldn't make out their words but could tell they were holding a council.

"*Kay na smey key fol ku lo.*" (We think you've betrayed our agreement.)

Peter dug his feet into the ground and spoke with indignation. "*Wey koo fee li naw.*" (I've done no such thing.)

They deliberated again, and Peter searched the woods around him to make sure no one witnessed his exchange. He glared at the band of mermaids, dauntless and unaffected by their deliberation. Peter held fast to the agreement he'd made with them. They'd keep Peter's device for him, and the next time the pirates had a conflict with the mermaids, Peter would help rather than remain neutral.

"*Key mi fey na si bel le pirates.*" (You've been seen with the pirates.)

"*Ya, sy wey na fi la tey.*" (Yes, but I have not betrayed our agreement.)

The Tally Man must have told the mermaids about Peter's last visit to Black Cavern. Anger threatened to consume him. If the Tally Man's big mouth cost Peter his chance to retrieve his age calculator, he'd be reconsidering all alliances.

"*Wey be na fel men mes so pirates.*" (You should know better than to associate with pirates.)

Peter bit his lip to avoid calling them a bunch of hypocrites. They were the ones who let the pirates use their passage to return to Neverland from Earth.

"*Es key men se ba lee, wey mi es enso di.*" (If you want it, you'll have to come and get it.)

The orangish mermaid retreated with the device, leaving Peter to face the rest alone. If he let the age calculator go, he'd have Sven to answer to. Hot rage filled Peter's chest. So much for controlling his emotions. He gave in to the feeling, allowed it to consume him. He'd need all the strength he could muster to fight off so many. His eyes narrowed in on a maroon mermaid. For some reason, Peter selected her as the one he would kill if it came to that. He hoped it wouldn't. Though the creatures were fierce, their rock spears would not be a match for the knife Peter carried.

Peter took off his leather jacket and dove into the water. Rather than fight first, he swam after the one keeping his possession. Before long, two mermaids had grabbed his feet. Peter began to kick, already needing to get to the surface for air. The mermaids let him go—their way of teasing their prey. They'd let him catch a breath and then pull him down again.

Peter gulped for air too soon and gagged on a mouthful of water. He sputtered and coughed. Two new mermaids came after him, grabbing his arms and pulling him down. Peter struggled, slipping one arm free and jabbing one of the mermaids in the nose. She pulled back, dropping her spear and holding onto her wound. The other continued to drag Peter down, now joined by the previous two. Peter heard a faint splash. Distracted by a commotion, the mermaids turned from Peter. He kicked them away and swam to the surface again for a breath.

Peter looked toward the shore and saw Karl fighting the band of mermaids. From the corner of his eye, Peter caught sight of an orangish creature moving underwater. He seized his chance and swam after the mermaid, catching her in her flight to help her sisters.

Peter struggled to pull the device from her grasp, but glanced at her face, noticing a look of indecision. She glanced away from Peter, as if the others called to her. He thought she probably wanted to go help them rather than fight Peter alone. Sometimes the mermaids working in unison served as an advantage to their enemies. She let go of the dial and swam away. After catching his breath, Peter headed for the shore.

"Peter, help," Karl called.

Peter shoved the dial deep into his wet pocket and began swimming toward the clash until he heard a mermaid's cry. The wailing broke all other sounds. The noise rent Peter's heart. Though they were cruel, Peter hated to see Neverland creatures die.

"That's enough, Karl. Let them go," Peter called.

The mermaids retreated, and their sister sank to the bottom of the lake.

Karl struggled for breath. "I did it, Peter. I killed a mermaid."

The pride in Karl's voice disturbed Peter. "Well done," Peter said. "Thank you for coming, but I told you to go back."

Karl slapped his hand on the water, splashing a pool of liquid into Peter's face. "You're welcome." He looked toward the sky. "Woohoo!" he yelled.

"Karl, let's get out of the water." Peter grabbed the boy's shirt and pulled.

When they reached the shore, Karl sank to the ground. "That was amazing. Peter, did you see how they all swam away?"

"Yes, Karl. Here, take this." Peter handed Karl a sack of gold fairy dust. "It will help you dry out. There's plenty in there to let you fly back as well. You must go. Don't tell the others about any of this."

"Not tell? Yeah, that's likely. I just killed a mermaid!"

"Shut up!" Peter said. "It's nothing to be proud of."

"But Peter, now—"

"I said that's enough." A wave of shame washed over Peter as he remembered the mermaids he'd killed in his younger days.

"All right, fine." Karl wrapped his arms around his knees. "Why can't I tell the others? Shouldn't they know what happened?"

"I don't want them to worry. I need you to do something for me."

"What is it, Peter? You sound upset. What's happened? Have the pirates threatened you again? Or Charlie?"

"No, it's not that. But I need to go to Earth for a bit. I don't want the others to know."

"But why?"

"If they ask, tell them you saw me trading with the Tally Man."

Peter could feel the fairy dust taking effect. The water trickled from his clothes, leaving a stream at his feet that receded back to the lake. Karl began to appear dry as well.

"What's an age calculator?" Karl asked.

"Never mind," Peter said. "Do as I asked."

"Yes, mother." Karl stood, threw the bag of fairy dust into the air, and caught it again. He rolled his eyes at Peter and walked away.

After finding and dusting off his jacket, Peter became airborne and looked back over his shoulder, watching Karl shrink. A pit grew in Peter's stomach. The height didn't bother him, but the guilt did. Peter knew the

Lost Boys could sense something was wrong, but he continued to build a wall between himself and his tribe of fellow orphans.

The events of his last visit to Black Cavern flitted through Peter's mind. Thankfully, because of Neverland's effect on pain and memory, Peter had healed quickly and forgotten much of the experience. The things that stood out to him most were Charlie's presence, the fuss over the age calculator, and being branded on the shoulder. Still, Peter couldn't deny the consequences. He felt anxious almost constantly and had even suffered a few episodes that he thought were probably panic attacks. He began to feel more and more unsettled as he left Autumn Quarter and entered the realm of the pirates.

The pirate ship came into view, anchored near the shore where the cliffs of Black Cavern towered above Endal Ocean. Peter landed on the edge of one of the cliffs to scope out Sven's location before approaching. He lay down on the rocky floor. The sun shone brightly above him, and Peter wished he could feel its warmth.

Peter could hear faint chatter coming from below. He glanced toward the ship and saw three pirates conversing on the main deck. Sven appeared, emerging from his cabin along with his first mate. Sven glanced up at Peter, and Peter lowered his head, questioning his decision to comply with Sven's request. A spark of bravery caused Peter to lift his head once more. Just as Peter had suspected, Sven could see him and used the fingers of his right hand to beckon Peter.

Peter stood and jumped off the cliff, soaring toward the ship and landing a safe distance from Sven.

"So you've brought it? Hoping to live, are you?"

Peter took a deep breath and sighed. He glared at Sven, uncertain if he dared ask any more questions. Peter reached into his pocket and grasped his age calculator. In some ways, he'd come to view the device as his only link with reality. In other ways, it was a temptation, a pest that demanded his attention. Peter pulled the small object into view. He looked down at it and marveled at the technology. If he stayed on Neverland, his age remained frozen. Peter's age hadn't changed since his last trip to Earth.

"I'll be taking that now," Sven said, his palm cupped to receive Peter's offering.

Peter, however, wasn't sure he could part with it. He took in his surroundings: Sven's distance, the activity of the other pirates, the proximity of the plank, the sparkles shimmering on the water as far as he could see. Peter could escape if it came to that. He needed to know.

"What do you want with it?" Peter asked.

Sven lowered his head and took a step toward Peter. "You are a fool, Peter. You can't grow up. Not here."

"What do you mean?"

Sven looked Peter in the eye. "I won't let you. Little boys are easy enough to deal with, but I won't have a rivalry with someone so old. It makes things entirely too fair."

"I don't understand."

"Then let me spell it out for you. If you continue your trips to England, and reach the age of eighteen, I will give you two choices. You can die a free man. Or you can become a pirate. Aren't I a generous captain?"

Sven's first mate, Jack Raven, watched the exchange with interest, all the while wearing a giant smile. Peter wanted to go and smack the grin off Jack's face.

"You're no captain of mine," Peter said.

"But I may be one day. Give it here, Peter. Be a good boy." Sven took another step toward Peter.

A vision flashed in Peter's mind. He saw a girl. The image was faded, but Peter was certain this daydream was significant.

"Or," Sven began. "You could stop going to Earth and stay a Lost Boy forever."

A plum-colored fairy flew in front of Peter's face, mirroring the despair creeping up on him. He lowered his hand, twirling the age calculator as he deliberated. His daydream vanished, and Peter thought only of the so-called choices Sven had presented.

"What will it be?" Sven asked. "Either way, I'll be taking that instrument, so I know for sure what you choose."

Peter began to take note of the movement of the other pirates. It seemed they were preparing for a trip.

"Going somewhere?" Peter asked.

"That's none of your business, Peter. But I thank you for your inquiry." Sven gritted his teeth and spat, "Hand it over."

Peter knew that when Sven's angry side began to show, it was time to comply. He tossed the dial to his rival and lifted into the air before Sven could get any closer or have the others pounce him.

As Peter soared over the ocean, he allowed the daydream to return—his vision of a girl he didn't even know. He had two more trips to Earth—one temporary, the other permanent. He knew the pirates were planning a departure, and Peter would leave as soon as they did. He had one month to spend on Earth. It didn't seem like enough time, but if he planned to leave Neverland forever, time was something he'd have to come to terms with.

London, 2015

The darkness of London's damp streets haunted Peter, reminding him of Black Cavern and Sven's threats. He shivered, barely able to focus on his plan or even enjoy the fact that he wasn't currently in Neverland. For decades he had come to Earth in an increasingly regular rhythm, trying to escape the loneliness that Neverland produced, but with the threats of the pirates hanging over his head, panic had also set in. He twitched as he strode across the bridge, taking in every sight and sound around him—not for pleasure, but to satisfy the paranoia. He didn't even know if the pirates were aware of his latest departure. Surely by now they would have noticed the numbers changing on his age calculator, and if they caught him, he'd be facing pirate torture again, or worse. Peter wasn't sure how Sven would go about turning him into a pirate, but he didn't want to find out. His last encounter had left him black and blue from head to toe, complete with a sizeable branding on his left shoulder—a thick circle around a star, the same symbol branded on the shoulder of every Neverland pirate. Without thinking, Peter took hold of the wound, as if to shield it from further pain.

Peter thought of how Karl's bravery had saved him from the mermaids, and of how proud Karl had been to kill one of them. Peter remembered tossing his sole possession at his greatest rival and leaving Neverland after watching the pirates leave first. He felt safer knowing they wouldn't be a threat to the Lost Boys since Sven and his band usually took extended trips to Earth.

By the shrewd trading of some fairy dust with the Tally Man, Peter was able to secure enough money to survive for several weeks in London. But the weeks drained by, and it had only been a few days since Peter spotted her. By now he knew where she lived and where she went to school. He'd learned by watching her interact with peers at school that her name was Jane. He also knew she volunteered at a child care center every afternoon, which was where he'd first spied her jumping in puddles with the children as they waited for their parents to arrive. He'd also seen her eating red gelatin on her way home. In short, she was perfect for Neverland: old enough to take care of the others but still young at heart. The Lost Boys would love her, especially Charlie, who still longed for a mother and was obsessed with red gelatin, even though the Tally Man rarely traded such things.

Unable to push through his nerves over the idea of approaching her, Peter simply followed her around. He couldn't imagine why she was out walking at night. Not that he minded so much. Watching her travel to school and waiting outside her house proved fruitless. Peter's fear of speaking with her kept thwarting his plan. Now that she walked alone out in the open, he determined to take advantage of the opportunity. It might be his only one. Peter recalled the times he'd caught a glimpse of her through the day care window. As the cars rushed by on the busy street and the rain drizzled down over Peter's cheeks, there she was—always smiling, always holding a baby or playing a game with one of the small children. He hated to admit it, but she'd done something to his heart already—pricked it somehow. He couldn't quite say, but he'd become attached to the idea of choosing *her*. Bringing her back with him was part of his escape plan now, as if she was the girl from the vision.

Peter slowed when he saw her walk toward a ticket booth at Kensington Olympia Station. He'd been so careful not to let her see him, and he didn't want to ruin that now. Somehow the thought of approaching her and striking up a conversation in which he would invite her to come with him to another planet frightened him even more than murderous pirates. He slipped under the pedestrian overpass and sat down on a bench, making sure the few faces gracing the station did not belong to any pirates he knew. He couldn't let her see the pirates; if she knew the danger, she might not come with him, and his chances were slim enough.

Peter sighed and leaned his head back, looking up at the bland underbelly of the overpass, fighting the urge to shut his heavy eyelids. Sleep threatened to take him, and his senses began to dull until someone sat next to him. Peter jerked to the side, moving about a foot away, ready to bolt if necessary. His heart jumped into a frenzy. To his vast surprise, it was not Sven or one of the other pirates. It was Jane, the girl he'd been following. He stared at her, noticing the smooth skin of her face as she unabashedly stared at him in return.

"What's your problem?" she asked.

"You . . ." Breathless, all Peter could do was point at her and stutter. "You . . . you . . ."

"I'm your problem? Is that why you've been following me, Stalker Boy?"

So much for the first impression. Peter's face began to burn, and a cold sweat leaked from under his arms. He'd been certain she didn't have a clue about his distant attention, and now that she was calling him out, the embarrassment churned in his chest, causing a sudden dizziness and giving him a craving for salty foods. His instinct told him to find the nearest hole and climb on down, but he would have to come up with something to say if any chance for a second impression remained.

"How'd you know I was following you?" Peter whispered in a raspy voice.

"I'm not an idiot, you know. But apparently you are. So, what's the deal? Were you planning to kill me and leave my dismembered remains somewhere? If you didn't know that I knew you were following me, I don't think you'd be able to get away with murder."

Such coolness. Such calm. Peter gawked in amazement. Her words completely contrasted with her attitude. If she truly thought him a stalker—or worse, a murderer—she didn't seem to care. Grabbing the entertainment section of a newspaper resting on the bench next to her, she lifted it and began to read as if she hadn't just stolen the breath away from him. Peter couldn't seem to get his jaw to cooperate; his mouth gaped wide, and there was nothing he could do about it. Perusing the paper, she pulled an apple from her bag and took a giant bite of it, juice bursting around her mouth.

Again, with the words. Peter couldn't think of any. Rather than attempt to speak, he studied her. Her dark brown hair was streaked with bright red highlights, and it was longer on one side—making it both chin-length and shoulder-length—which Peter found endearing. Endearment,

Peter mused, an emotion that turned Neverland fairies a soft blue at their centers and a glowing pastel yellow toward the edges, one of only a few feelings that produced two hues. Jane wore a dark green canvas jacket that covered up a graphic tee, along with a blue-and-white plaid pleated skirt. Her bare knees stood out above the pair of dark brown boots hugging her legs and ankles. Allowing her words to play back in his mind, he realized she didn't sound British. Flustered by this realization, Peter reconsidered his choice.

She turned away from the paper and focused on him. "So?" Her eyes widened mid-glare. "Wait a minute, do I know you? Do you go to Ashbourne too?"

All these inquiries swirled in Peter's head; he truly could handle only one question at a time. Ashbourne was her school, but he'd never stepped inside. Peter cleared his throat, hoping that would help him get a phrase out. Nope. Distracted by the color of her eyes, all he could muster was, "Facetious."

She leaned forward, lowering the paper to her lap. "Say what?"

"Your eyes . . ." Peter glanced around for a water fountain. His throat felt like the air in the Neverland desert, where it often reached temperatures above one hundred and forty degrees Fahrenheit. He tried clearing his throat again. "Your eyes . . . they're facetious."

What he meant to say was that they were the same color as a Neverland fairy who is feeling facetious—a glowing, walnut brown. Maybe he should stop reading his study journals. All his notes about Neverland fairies and their corresponding colors and emotions were not helping right now. Perhaps he needed to stop at the library and snag a book about how to converse with the opposite sex.

"Yeah. No idea what that means. So, why are you following me? Obviously you're not a murderer." She took a moment to size him up, seemingly unimpressed and absent of fear. Her words failed to pierce Peter in an accusing way at all. She sounded curious, as if she sincerely wanted to know. This almost gave him the courage.

"I . . . I . . ." Peter ran his fingers through his hair, suddenly conscious of the fact that he hadn't looked in a mirror for days. Then he thought of how weird it was that days existed on Earth and not in Neverland. Perhaps this girl thought he looked like a crazy person. He turned to glance at his reflection in a window. Sometimes it surprised him how old he looked, and other times it seemed he looked much younger than he felt inside. Surprised to see a stuttering teenaged boy, Peter took note of his disheveled appearance. His brown hair stuck up in several places, and he'd grown a bit fuzzy around his jaw and chin. One side of his jacket collar was sticking up, and the other was where it should be. His own eyes reminded him of a silvery-blue fairy, the color for contentment.

"Look, my train leaves in fifteen minutes. I'm not sure I've got enough time to hear whatever it is you can't seem to say." She set the paper to her side again, her eyes lingering on the headlines.

"Where are you going?" he asked.

She shrugged. "Anywhere."

It was now or never. "Come away with me." Peter fought the urge to clasp his hand over his mouth, but he couldn't help widening his eyes at the shock of hearing his own statement, and it took several seconds before he realized his jaw stretched well below its usual position. He burned in his leather jacket—even with the wet chill in the air—and as a figure passed in front of them, Peter was reminded of the danger he may be in.

She faced him again, looking appalled. "Excuse me? You're a creep. A dumb one. I'm not going anywhere with you."

Needing a change of scene to gather his thoughts, Peter stood up and speed walked around the corner, hoping her curiosity would lead her to follow him. He tried to console himself that even if the pirates knew he'd left Neverland, he was in London, hidden in a sea of eight million people. It wouldn't be easy for Sven to find him. Peter took a deep breath and released the air, trying to let go of the fear as well.

The station rumbled with motion as a train approached. Peter envisioned what it would be like to watch her board the train and pull away. He'd followed her for nothing. The details of their brief encounter swirled about in Peter's mind. There was much more to this female than a love of children and a penchant for red gelatin. He half expected her to come after him in self-defense and then leave *his* dismembered remains somewhere.

A familiar phrase popped into Peter's head, one that Bryson used often: "When you can't decide what to do, let fate choose for you." Bryson's constant battle with indecision often left Peter and the other Lost Boys to endure meals of inventive combinations such as "eel au gratin" and "pickle ice cream." Jane had not followed him. Peter offered a little prayer to fate, asking for a small sign. He would let the train move on, and if Jane happened to still be there after it pulled away, then she was destined for Neverland. If she boarded the train and sped away from him, he would look for another. Leaving-on-a-train-Jane. That's how he thought of her then. He wondered where she was going but accepted that he would probably never know.

Peter noticed a newspaper clipping pinned on a bulletin board. It was the same article Jane had been reading only moments before, featuring tabloid-like pictures, one of a man and one of a woman. The caption read: "Actors Stuart Landing and Vicki Schwartz confirmed their separation Tuesday. Hollywood's sweetheart couple plan to divorce after twenty years of marriage."

He couldn't help thinking of his own parents, the ones he'd ran away from more than a century ago. He'd learned of their deaths decades too late. He'd obsessed over the years about what had ever happened to them and the torments he had most likely caused. Perhaps their own marital relationship had been forever altered by his decision to leave them for an eternity of youthful adventures and frivolity.

Peter tried to ignore the fading sounds of motion as the train pulled out.

"Lovely couple, aren't they?"

Peter jerked around after hearing the feminine echo, landing his eyes on a sight that was both reassuring and nerve-racking. "Do you think so?"

"They're my parents."

"Seriously?"

Peter returned his gaze to the article. A pit grew in his stomach when a thought crossed his mind. Peter was a Lost Boy. He could see the signs. He faced her once more. "Are you running away?"

"Not exactly."

"Leaving-on-a-train-Jane."

"I'm not sure I'm ever going to understand you, but do you have like fifteen pounds I could borrow?"

He reached into his pocket to feel the last few pounds and coins. "No," Peter replied, both disheartened that he couldn't help her and elated that she stood facing him in all her boldness. "I thought you were leaving."

"Yeah, well I intended to when I came here. Forgot my wallet though. I just told you I was leaving because I wanted to deter your murder plans."

A laugh escaped Peter's lips, the first he'd let out in ages. "I'm not going to kill you. Actually, I'm pathetically harmless." Unless of course you were a dangerous pirate or a selfish mermaid that needed to be dealt with.

"So, what's your name?" Jane asked.

Peter forced a deep breath while deciding how honest he could be with her. She seemed fearlessly honest in a way he could never hope to be. Still, he couldn't shake the feeling that she deserved the truth in this point at least.

"I'm Peter Pan."

Her expression changed from curiosity to bitter disappointment. "Mary Poppins. Nice to meet you." She curtsied, adjusted the strap of her bag on her shoulders and turned away.

Clearly, she knew about Peter's fictionalizations. It boosted his ego to know his name was still getting around, but he flinched as desperation took control and forced him to say something stupid again. "I'll take you to a magical place. One where there is endless beauty and wonder."

"I don't do drugs," she called without looking back, waving a hand in dismissal as she hurried toward the street. "Thanks for nothing."

"What is wrong with me?" Peter asked, burying his forehead in his hand. But fate had chosen her. She hadn't left on the train. He wouldn't lose hope, not while he still had breath and at least some remaining intelligence.

Peter caught up with her, determined not to let anything idiotic come out of his mouth. "Why didn't you get on the train?"

"Left my wallet at home, Stalker Boy. Will you please leave me alone? You're seriously starting to annoy me," she said.

"I'll get it for you," Peter said.

"I'm perfectly capable. Obviously." She continued, and all the while, no part of their conversation dissuaded her from her determination.

Peter watched her for a moment, noticing the way her dark hair bobbed with her quick movements. "No really, let me go and get it for you. It will only take a few minutes." Peter touched her arm, the canvas material of her jacket damp from the mist. Knowing it would be more impressive if he ran first, Peter sprinted ahead of her. A smile came to his face as the adrenaline coursed through his body. Flying came as naturally as breathing, so Peter had little cause to run, but he couldn't deny it added a thrill. Peter glanced around to make sure nobody else would see. Anticipation built with each hard, swift movement until he could wait no longer. He lifted off the ground, traveling at the same speed but without the effort of running. Closer and closer to the stars he flew, spinning into a flip or two or three for nothing but the fun of it. He glanced back and thought he saw a stunned look on Jane's distant face. Not even the prospect of impressing—or perhaps even further frightening—Jane could deter the childish joy consuming him. Peter let out a howl of delight, the longing for childhood rushing back to him in one instant.

But it was too late for that. Peter was almost a man. The thought slowed him, both calming him and bringing a state of mild despair. Peter looked to the world below him. The sidewalks were damp and dark. Few vehicles made their way down the residential streets on the way to Jane's house. Only the sound of rushing wind could be heard at Peter's altitude. He passed through white clouds of mist, the air and rain cool on his cheeks. He closed his eyes for a moment, thoughts of escaping his current life and protecting the Lost Boys causing conflicting emotions. He imagined a disoriented fairy and opened his eyes once more and found Jane's house was near. Peter landed on her window sill.

His mood lightened upon inspecting Jane's bedroom. A bulletin board covered in pictures hung above her disheveled, rusty-orange bedding. Magazine collage art decorated her walls, one collage in the shape of a whale, one a cloud, and the last a guitar. Ball-shaped, bold-colored lanterns dangled from the ceiling. And there on the dresser sat her wallet, which, judging by its thickness, contained just enough for one train ticket to anywhere, or perhaps a credit card. A cell phone sat nearby, and it jumped into a buzz, startling Peter. A light began to flash along with a notice: 17 new messages. He debated taking the phone as well as the wallet but, since she hadn't mentioned it, left it untouched.

Though not his first time flying through a girl's window, Peter couldn't shake the jitters. He felt as though he stood on a balance beam, unable to steady himself and likely to falter. He wiped his palms on his jeans and wondered if his tolerance for fairy dust was turning into an immunity. The magical substance usually lifted his spirits enough to steady him and give him a reprieve from strong emotions. Perhaps his nervousness had nothing to do with the fairy dust or his immunity to it. He pictured Jane and recalled her words, and suddenly he understood the source of his agitation. This girl was so unique, so different from Wendy of old, who had been the epitome of motherly grace and refinement. As the idea took shape, Peter knew it to be true. He was afraid of her but thought it dangerous to explore the reasons and left it at that. In comparison, Peter had to admit that Jane really had only two things in common with Wendy: she enjoyed children, and she kept her window open.

Peter grabbed the wallet and headed for the window, becoming worried Jane would have gotten tired of waiting and vanished by now. He flew straight back to the station where he found Jane sitting on the same bench, her bag resting beside her.

He held out Jane's wallet. She reached for it as he finally got right to the point. "Jane, I know somewhere you could go. Come to Neverland with me?"

She sat motionless, except to grasp the wallet. "You're pretty convincing." Her voice sounded as though it carried a sorrow of its own. Time would smooth all that out: explain it to Peter and mend it for Jane. For now, they had to leave.

"But you're still leaving on that train?"

She shrugged. "I don't know. I was sort of thinking that since you're my hallucination, we should stick together."

The corners of Peter's mouth pulled upward. "Neverland is as good a place as any and far better than most."

Unaffected, she stared at Peter. He didn't dare hope. He straightened his lips once more, not wanting to come across as smug or flirtatious.

Despite his effort, Peter couldn't prevent one side of his mouth from curving upward. How long had it been since he'd been face-to-face with a girl? Whenever visiting Earth, he watched people constantly, but approached them only when necessary. "Have I at least convinced you I'm not a murderer?"

"I never thought you capable of that." Her scoffing and laughter stung a bit, though Peter bit his cheek to keep from laughing along with her. He didn't need to defend his pride here. Not now.

"This might help you make up your mind."

Peter reached into his pocket, allowing a large amount of fairy dust to fall into the palm of his hand. He pulled it out and held it in front of her, watching it shimmer in the darkness, the golden, glowing color of pure joy.

Looking intrigued, she stood and swung her backpack over her shoulder. "Is that . . . ? No, it can't be." She shook her head.

"What else would it be? It will allow you to come with me, but sadly, it won't take your pain away. Not completely. I imagine anyone willing to up and run away from home has had their share of pain."

She ignored him, keeping her focus on the bright, shimmering dust in his hand. He could sense she wanted to reach out and touch it. Her hand lifted slightly but went no farther.

"Will you come with me? Since you need somewhere to go anyway?"

"What will happen to me?"

"That will be entirely up to you." Peter had his ideas, but he would never force her to stay in Neverland.

"Aren't there pirates in Neverland?"

To deny that would be a bold lie. Just a smidgen of deception in a spoonful of truth. No more. Peter wouldn't allow it to go any further. "Don't tell me you're afraid of some adventure."

"Not afraid. Just not stupid." Even while Jane looked him in the eye, her hand inched closer to the pile of golden dust he held out to her.

"I promise that Neverland is perfectly safe." Which was sort of true. If she stayed close to him, it would be safe. He could teach her the ropes, get her all situated, make sure the pirates left her alone . . . somehow. Then he could leave for good.

"And this will make me fly, I suppose? Is that how you get to your island?"

"Neverland is not an island."

"Oh, right, it's a star."

"Well, there are stars, but Neverland is actually a planet."

She appeared to be mulling all this over, her eyes intent as the wheels in her head spun round and round. "Hmm. And will I have to think happy thoughts? Because I'm not having a lot of those right this second." She seemed more entranced, and Peter knew the effects of the dust were beginning. It would take a great force of will for her to resist the temptation of Neverland now.

"Happy thoughts are optional. Some say they help, but the fairy dust is powerful enough with or without them."

"Why are you so old? You must be at least sixteen. Isn't Peter Pan a child?"

Peter looked around him to make sure they were still alone. It was getting late, and Peter realized how fateful it had been to approach her at night when the streets were nearly empty. Even the ticket booth was now closed.

"I'll answer that question and any others you have if you only come with me."

Peter watched as her fingertips pinched a tiny spot of golden dust, sealing her fate.

"Look down," he said.

Jane gasped when she found that her feet had lifted several inches off the ground and she floated in midair. She laughed and began kicking her legs, as if that would help with anything. "How is this possible?"

Relief swept across him, so complete and foreign he couldn't remember the last time he'd experienced it so fully. He branded the moment into his memory. Aquamarine, the color of relief. Jane in Neverland. Everything was going to be fine.

TAKING FLIGHT

*D*riven by a sense of urgency, Peter suppressed his nerves and reached out his hand to Jane, hoping she would trust enough to take it.

"Take my hand," Peter pleaded, finding the paranoia sneaking up on him again.

The tip of her index finger brushed against his palm before she clasped tight in response to the alarm she must be feeling, her hold stretching and pulling his skin. Peter held firm, eager to lead her away. Her legs moved as if she were in water, circling about even though Peter knew that wouldn't help.

"Just hold still," he said, subduing a laugh. "Let the dust do the balancing for you. Just let go of any worry and trust the process." He held her hand—warm in the frightened chill of his own—pulling slightly as they ascended and moved away from the overpass and toward the night sky. They rose above the train station, the embankment and even all of London soon becoming visible. Peter kept aware of the scenes below, hoping no one would notice them, but it wouldn't be long before he and Jane disappeared into the darkness, far above any light bright enough to reveal them on this moonless night.

Peter looked at Jane, witnessing several emotions—joy, excitement, wonder, amazement—but not fear.

"This is crazy," Jane yelled, shaking her head in disbelief. Speaking softer, she followed up with, "And incredible." She pointed with her free hand, looking as though she longed to put her feet back on the ground, her toes reaching downward again and again. Still, she basked in the sights. "There's the London Eye. And I think I can already see Windsor Castle.

The country is so dark at night." Her free arm waved about, not quite the flap of a bird's wing, but seemingly deliberate nonetheless. "It's all so small now. We must be traveling faster than an airplane, and yet . . ." Her face sobered. "Peter, won't we burn up? I mean leaving Earth's atmosphere? Won't that kill us?" She kept tugging him by the hand in her attempts to gain control of her balance.

Jane would learn all the magic of fairy dust eventually. "No, Jane. We're safe." He had never known anyone so trusting and perhaps so venturesome since Wendy. Jane would need that sense of adventure.

A twinge of guilt flared as Peter questioned whether he was doing the right thing. He had brought Jane with the intent to win her trust, show her the glories of Neverland, convince her that she was vital to its future and that remaining was imperative, and then leave her behind. She beamed in the faint starlight, ignorant of his objectives. Peter grimaced.

As they continued to move upward, their speed increased, the fairy dust forming a streaking gold blockade against the dangers and pollutions of earth's atmosphere. Only a moment and a gentle burst later, they floated in the great dark of space. As far as Peter had been able to discover, the blockade also served as an oxygen bubble, somehow allowing breathing to occur normally.

Jane laughed now, otherwise speechless. Peter relaxed for a moment, catching his breath and enjoying the celestial view. Flying took zero effort without gravity's pull, and Jane seemed more at ease as well. Peter reminisced about the many times he had been through the fairy portal—available anywhere along Earth's circumference after reaching the exosphere (as long as fairy dust was a factor anyway).

It amazed him every time how there could be such colorful brightness floating about in a sea of black. It reminded him of the fairies, bursts of color in the shadow of Neverland.

"This way," Peter said, leading Jane onward to the wormhole.

"What's that?" Jane asked, apprehension in her voice as she gestured toward the apparent void.

Peter had to admit, the wormhole that currently gave access to Neverland was more frightening than previous ones, even for him. A swirl of blue and pink led downward over a sheer cliff into blackness.

"It's the way to Neverland. Don't worry. It only takes a moment, and it's actually quite exhilarating."

Her hand squeezed his, and she glanced back at Earth before bravely looking into the hole again.

"Ready?" Peter asked.

She nodded, though he could tell her courage faded. Peter led them in feetfirst, knowing a head dive usually produced more adverse side effects, like severe vertigo and plaguing nausea that seemed to last forever in a place where time was unmeasurable.

Another burst of speed sucked them out of their position in the Milky Way and shot them through a giant tube of blackness surrounded by streaks of glowing color. After all these years, the ride still gave Peter a nervous tickle in his gut, and he loved it. A sadness struck him though, replacing the excitement. This could be his last time traveling to Neverland. Barely aware of Jane and her attempt to keep from squealing, Peter's melancholy distraction flitted away as soon as he could see the literal light at the end of the tunnel. One final swoop, as if the wormhole opening on Neverland's end were spitting them out, and there it was: only a dark sphere at first, but growing brighter as the brightest Never stars shed light on her glory. In only a moment the details became more visible.

Peter looked at Jane again to find her shaking her head, eyes shut tight. She resembled someone trying to determine if they were dreaming or not. Staring at her, he began to wonder if a dream beguiled *him*. Jane seemed beyond hope and reason. Airplane-Jane, he mused, smiling at the awkward way she tried to establish grace in the air. Fate had been generous to him today.

Peter pointed out High Mountain as they rounded Autumn Quarter and entered Winter Quarter. The peaks of the mountain towered over the land below, making everything surrounding it—a lake, a forest, an open plain, and several hills—appear fairy sized. Neverland Pointed trees dotted patches of the mountain, and snow glistened in the turquoise moonlight. As they continued toward Spring Quarter and approached land, Tower Lake and the Northern Forest came into view as well; Peter located his Neverland hollow tree. Before landing, though, he would give her a tour.

"Open your eyes," he told her. Her hand felt clammy now and cool in his.

She obeyed, and what wonder! Maybe humans didn't change color as Neverland fairies did, but their emotions were still decipherable. Peter tried to picture Jane as grandly miniscule, with a fairy body, and in a magnificent shade of purple-blue.

Shadow Valley rested in the center of Summer Quarter, sunken and shadowed. It was made of dark, jagged rock and void of all plant life, giving Peter and the Lost Boys little reason to visit. Peter led Jane over the Southern Desert, followed by the sandy, pristine shores of Endal Ocean. They descended so low that they were dampened by the spray of ocean waves on their faces.

"This is incredible," Jane said, closing her eyes again as they glided across the water.

Circling around the planet once more, Peter and Jane returned to the winter lands of High Mountain. The vast evergreen forest surrounding the mountain was blanketed in snowy white.

"Are the seasons more constant here somehow? It looks like there are four sections."

"Yes," Peter replied with enthusiasm, impressed with how quickly she caught on. "The seasons never change here within and related to regions. So, winter is always available if you're willing to travel to it. The planet spins *with* its sun and moon as opposed to the celestial bodies spinning around each other. The Lost Boys and I live in Spring Quarter."

Jane smirked as though she didn't quite believe him. "And the pirates, where do they live?"

"Summer Quarter." Peter hadn't noticed the pirate ship, having avoided the cliffs outside Black Cavern. The idiots were probably still trying to earn passage back. The Tally Man could be hard to find. The pirates rarely had enough fairy dust to fly back to Neverland and used alternative methods to return after visiting Earth.

Hollow Tree Wood came into view again, and Peter led Jane downward, slowing just before they reached the ground.

They landed, Peter having become so comfortable with Jane's hand in his he couldn't feel it anymore. That is, until she pulled it away.

"I am dreaming, right?" she asked, placing one hand to her sweaty forehead and using the other for balance. She shifted on her feet, as though she might fall over or pass out, and her face paled suddenly.

Concern for her grew, although Peter knew a little flight sickness normally overwhelmed first-time visitors. "Jane, are you all right? You look pale."

She sat down on a nearby rock, seemingly unaware of the Lost Boys who began coming out of their trees to greet them. "I think I'm gonna be sick. Go ahead and turn around. I don't want you to see me barf."

"Who is she, Peter?" Lester asked, sporting his usual T-shirt and cut-off jeans. He wiped his hands on a cloth.

"Who is she?"

"Yeah, who is she?"

Voice after voice sounded, asking questions and murmuring to the others.

Peter couldn't turn away from her. She needed him. "Come rest in the Elder Hollow tree."

"The what?" Jane placed a fist on her right hip and pressed a hand to her mouth as if trying to keep the contents of her stomach down. She leaned forward, looking more pea green now, the color fairies turned when they truly were sick.

"Peter, bring her inside," Bryson said, stepping toward them. "Or do you think we should leave her?"

Peter gently placed his hand under her elbow and helped her up. She swayed on her feet and her mouth shot open. A pile of what appeared to be chopped-up carrot chunks in a liquid goop landed on his suede shoes.

A cry of disgust erupted from the crowd, and even little Misty began to gag, as if she might add to the pile of puke. "I've never had the strongest stomach, Peter," the little girl said. "Remember when I first came?"

"Yes, Misty. Hopefully Jane will not be sick for seven different shades of moon like you were."

"Her name's Jane?" Simon asked. Unlike his twin sister, Misty, sickness never took hold of little Simon. Peter glanced at them with adoration. He could detect the similarity in their mannerisms and graces even when they did something as simple as watch the infirm. Though their actions gave away their relation, their appearance did not. Simon's dark hair looked nothing like the swirly, auburn mop atop Misty's head. The girl had freckles. The boy did not. The boy's lanky figure contrasted with the girl's round features. But they acted the same. Where had it come from, mother or father? Or perhaps it was simply from a need to remain as close to one another as possible after coming to Neverland.

"Here," Lester said as he held out a cloth to Jane. None of the other Lost Boys volunteered to help her. But Lester, probably because he stood in the position of the eldest Lost Boy (besides Peter), had to offer something, set some kind of example, and show welcome in some manner at least. He stared at Peter now and held up his palms as if asking Peter what this was all about.

Peter began to feel queasy himself, more from all the questions than the wormhole. He'd been a bit distant ever since Sven had branded his shoulder, and he knew the Lost Boys could tell. Lester kept close watch over Peter, but even Lester remained uninformed as to Peter's plans. Only Karl knew about Peter traveling to Earth, and gratefully, it seemed he'd kept the information to himself as Peter had asked.

"You went to the Mother Land?" Lester asked, referring to Earth. "Karl told us you were busy bartering with the Tally Man."

"I never found the Tally Man. I'm sorry." Peter would keep changing the subject if he had to. If only they knew how valuable Jane would prove.

Shaking himself from his thoughts, Peter noticed Jane attempting to stand.

"I think I'll be okay," she said.

"Let's take her to the Elder Hollow. She'll need plenty of rest after that journey," Bryson said, ever wise when he could actually make up his mind.

Jane opened her mouth but faltered before saying anything. She simply nodded.

"Lester, help me lift her."

"I can walk," Jane muttered, but her eyes closed and her head fell back as she passed out. Peter caught her in his arms, and Lester and Bryson stepped forward to help carry her.

The three lifted her, Peter from behind and the others each taking a leg. They shuffled toward the Elder Hollow Tree, which housed a makeshift hospital on the lower level and a large meeting room on the level above.

Everyone watched, and Peter could not ignore the confused looks on their faces.

"Is she our new mother?" asked a brave, childish voice. Charlie's question chilled Peter's blood, although he couldn't exactly say why. Lester and Bryson stopped and turned to Peter.

"What does he mean?" Lester asked.

Of the current Lost Boys, none of them had ever read *Peter Pan* by J. M. Barrie, and only a couple had ever seen a movie or play telling the story. While they knew in general that Peter Pan was a name that came with Neverland and that someone named Wendy had been a part of that story long ago, they knew little else. Charlie's question had been the sincere longing of a young boy who innately understood his need for a mother.

Revealing his plan now seemed risky. What if Jane opted to leave Neverland? Yet, Peter couldn't let go of the hope helping him through every step. The hope that she would stay and, because of that, he could leave. While many of the others were quite capable, none of them were as old as Jane, whom Peter guessed was close to his own age. She had more real-life experience, and a naturally motherly disposition. Many of the Lost Boys were too egocentric still. Sure, putting them in charge would take care of that, but that's what happened to Peter, one of the reasons he became so disenchanted with the idea of eternal youth. Taking care of the others became too much responsibility. The older he became, the more he cared for their welfare, and the more his own inner child seeped away. He wanted the other Lost Boys to enjoy their childhoods for as long as possible. Jane could help accomplish that.

In a moment of impulse, Peter replied. "Yes, Charlie. She is your new mother."

Amid a noticeable silence from most of the Lost Boys, Peter nodded his head and pushed Jane's body to encourage Lester and Bryson forward. Entering the darkness of the Elder Hollow, Peter guided them toward the bed nearest the door.

"I'll stay with her until she wakes up. She'll probably be confused."

"Is she dead?" Frank asked.

"Yeah, is she dead?" Timothy echoed.

"No, boys. She'll be fine," Peter said, having personally felt a pulse underneath her arms as he carried her. Not that he'd been worried—nobody ever died from coming to Neverland.

"Peter, may I speak with you?" Lester asked, and Peter couldn't help noticing his confrontational tone.

"Of course," Peter replied softly. All their eyes watched him intently, some teeming with confusion, others with unasked questions. "Bryson, please take everyone back to their hollow trees. Lester and I will be in the meeting room upstairs. We won't be long."

Following Bryson's large body, the Lost Boys (and one Lost Girl) turned away from Peter and disappeared, Misty closing the door behind her.

Even through the thick door, Peter heard Charlie's whoop, "We have a mother!"

Lester turned away and climbed the spiral staircase. Peter followed, taking a few deep breaths in preparation.

When he reached the meeting room, Lester stood with his arms folded. "What's going on?" He leaned back slightly, his chin-length, dirty-blond hair framing his face. Lanky but strong, Lester had been a calming presence almost ever since he'd come to Neverland, but Peter knew Lester had his own leaving plans, a fact Peter wished he could ignore. In reality, though, Lester would probably leave first. Peter couldn't bear the thought of letting him go. He wondered who would start the fires. Nobody was as good at it as Lester.

Forced to make a quick decision about whether to play the idiot or fess up, Peter chose the latter. "Lester, I asked Karl to lie to you. I wasn't bartering with the Tally Man."

Lester snickered a bit. "I figured that much. But why, Peter? That's not like you. Ever since the pirates took you, you've been . . . different. Why did you bring her here?" Lester shifted his feet and waited for a response.

Trying to ignore the lump climbing his throat, Peter responded. "You're not the only one leaving. Someone must take care of them. Someone needs to take care of Neverland."

While Lester seemed to mull over the revelation, Peter realized he had never spoken his plans out loud before. He was surprised to discover that admitting it to someone brought a wave of relief and lightened his burden.

"When are you going to tell the others?"

A flicker of guilt sparked in Peter's mind. Telling the Lost Boys remained second on the list. Perhaps it wasn't even on the list at all. "I thought it'd be best to tell her first."

Lester smiled now, his conscience ever looser than Peter's. "She doesn't know? How in the Neverland stars did you ever get her to come with you?" He laughed a bit and then patted Peter on the back as if he'd accomplished some heroic feat.

"Fate." Peter couldn't help smiling in response to Lester's attitude. "A fair bit of persuasion. And a load of luck. I think this girl is lucky. The fairy dust didn't hurt either."

"I won't tell the others, Peter. I'll leave that to you."

"Thanks, Les. I think. Still planning to leave yourself?"

Lester nodded. Peter would miss him. Who could say if they'd ever cross paths on Earth? They'd discussed it at length. Lester planned to turn himself in to the Bristol child protection authorities. Being an orphan, he would need a foster family until he reached adulthood. Keeping in contact seemed unlikely.

"Just let me know when you're ready. Say the word and we'll get it over with."

Lester nodded. "Now, what about the Tally Man? When are you going to get us some chocolate? We've been out ever since Bryson experimented with making a chocolate lasagna."

"Let's get Jane settled. Then I'll try finding the Tally Man."

How the Lost Boys loved chocolate! Except for Karl. The most rugged of the group by far, he'd eat dirt before eating chocolate.

For the first time in ages, Peter caught a glimpse of freedom. In fact, he thought he could almost smell it. And after smelling comes tasting. And after tasting there is no going back.

"It's going to break their hearts, you know," said Lester.

A Neverland fairy experiencing acceptance turned a lavender gray. Peter imagined that color, fighting for that state of being.

"I know." But knowing and accepting often stood on parallel planes. If Peter expected to have peace eventually, he needed to find a way to make them intersect.

Waking in a Tree

*P*eter watched the rise and fall of Jane's chest. Never ginger sheets
and a dark wool blanket lay across her shoulders. A rosy color in
her cheeks replaced the paleness. He couldn't wait to get to know the girl
he'd brought to Neverland with him. Then suspicion replaced his excitement. What was her story? Running away from home, going with a perfect
stranger . . . Perhaps Jane had not been the right choice. And now it was
too late to change his mind.

Jane stirred, twisting and turning until the covers, which once flaw-
lessly rested on top of her, became a rumple of wrinkled bedding. Peter
smiled when he noticed how messy her hair looked. Endearing once again.
He took a mental snapshot, hoping it would last until he had the chance to
sketch the picture before him.

"Where am I?" Jane asked after sitting up.

"You're in the Elder Hollow. This is where we take care of anyone who
is sick." Peter realized this had a double meaning. While it was in fact the
tree they used to treat sickness, the tree was also sick itself, and would be
dying soon. He noted that finding a new hollow tree to act as their hospital
would be necessary. Perhaps even before he left.

Jane cast her eyes on Peter. Those brown eyes widened as if the memories from the station and their flight to Neverland came rushing back
anew. "You're that stalker boy from the train station." Her face took on a
different demeanor; Jane could have been fiery red-orange, the color for
an indignant fairy. "You abducted me." Surprise mingled with the anger
in her tone.

Quick to defend himself, Peter worked to calm her. "Now hold on a minute." He held his hands up toward her. "I did not abduct you. You came willingly. I offered fairy dust, and you took it. I offered my hand, and you took it. We began to fly." He paused for effect, narrowing his eyes at her. "And *you* enjoyed it." Finished with his speech, he lowered his hands. It seemed to be working. Pride replaced the nervousness he'd encountered when talking with her in London. She was in his element now, and he had the upper hand. She would need him to survive here, and this gave him a confidence he hadn't been able to find when approaching her initially.

She pondered for a moment. Lifting her eyebrows and shrugging her shoulders a bit, she gave up the battle with, "Touché."

She smiled at him next, which put him even more at ease. "Peter Pan," she breathed while shaking her head, as if she didn't quite believe it still.

"Leaving-on-a-train-Jane." This forced a question to his mind, his doubts not settling completely. "Where were you going anyway?" He thought of the newspaper article and her famous parents, but he wouldn't mention any of that.

She shrugged, dropping her eyes to inspect the sheets. "I told you—anywhere." She brought a fistful of sheet to her nose and sniffed. "These sheets smell like ginger."

"Yes, they do. No matter how many times you wash them. Drives Preston bonkers. Never did care for Never ginger."

"What is Never ginger?"

"It's a plant that can be used in cooking, or if you smash it and peel away the fibers, you can make thread. The materials made from that thread last forever. The Tally Man brings us sheets now, but these have been around for decades. We call it Never ginger because it's native, and because it smells and tastes a lot like ginger root."

Jane held the sheets to her face, closing her eyes and seeming to marvel over their softness.

"Pretty amazing, aren't they? Wait until you see the fairies."

"That's right," she said, dropping the sheets, her eyes wide in wonder once more. "I get to meet Tinker Bell!"

Peter chuckled at her enthusiasm. If only Tinker Bell truly existed, or any such fairy. "Tinker Bell was an exaggeration of Never fairies. They aren't nearly so much like humans." He could see the disappointment in her face and felt bemused for a moment that she was not changing colors. Disappointment brought a gray-blue hue to Never Fairies. "Think firefly with a bit of personality. The only one remotely close to Tinker Bell would be the queen, but it's rare to see the queen Never fairy. Besides, the current fairy queen and I don't relate well. She's a bit too moody for me."

Peter retrieved a cup of water from a nearby table and encouraged Jane to drink. She looked at it first, performing an inspection of sorts.

"It's perfectly safe. Taken from the Never spring and cooled in the underground ice cellar."

Convinced, or perhaps simply too thirsty to resist any longer, Jane drank. Peter took the cup from her and placed it back on the table.

"Hasn't it always been the same queen? I mean, wouldn't she live forever? This is Neverland."

Peter had never really thought about it like that. Neverland was such an eternal, unchangeable world. Sure, things could die, but they aged much slower than anything on Earth. And humans seemed not to age at all. Honestly, he couldn't remember how often a new queen took over.

"No, I remember several queens. Some brighter than others. Some more vain. Some a little ditzy."

"Seriously?" Jane asked.

Peter nodded, remembering fondly the queen that would come out of her nest, begin flying in one direction, change colors and switch directions, change colors once more, switch directions once more, and fly back into her nest. All the fairies turned the color of confusion whenever in her presence.

"And who's Preston? The one who doesn't like ginger?"

"He is the Lost Boy who knows his own mind. He's a bit quiet though, until you get to know him. Eyes bright as the Never blue sky. Dark hair. Always wearing green."

"That should make it easy to remember him."

Peter watched Jane shift in her bed. She seemed nervous, and Peter wondered if he'd done something to rattle her.

"Would you like to meet them?"

"I thought you'd never ask."

At this, the door burst open and in spilled a tumultuous pile of Lost Boys. Rather than focus on their (hopefully permanent) guest, the

Lost Boys focused on each other, either punching and accusing or timidly whispering to the person standing next to him. Little Charlie braved a glance first.

Looking at Jane, he directed his question at Peter. "Is this her, Peter?"

Wanting to cut him off before he mentioned the "M" word, Peter rushed to grab him. "Yes, Charlie. This is Jane. A brave and adventurous girl who came to Neverland for a spell."

"But I thought—" Charlie began.

Peter quickly moved to whisper in his ear. "Let's not scare her off by calling her 'Mother' yet. Agreed?"

Charlie's pudgy cheeks jiggled as he nodded, looking at Peter with those milk-chocolate eyes. Thinking about food sometimes made Peter hungry, no matter the context. Looking around the room, Peter noticed everyone had calmed. Lester gave Peter a reassuring nod. Given that gesture and the fact that nobody else seemed to be mentioning the "M" word, Peter figured Lester had asked them not to think of her in that way yet.

"I'm starved," Peter said. His stomach groaned and rumbled, not having received nourishment for too long. Eating in Neverland seemed optional sometimes and carried less necessity than eating on Earth. Perhaps visiting the Mother Land had triggered an onslaught of hunger.

"I made breakfast, Peter." Bryson—who they lovingly referred to as Bryson the Bison given his large size—insisted on making square meals regularly and always rotated between breakfast, lunch, and dinner.

"What do you say, Jane?" Peter asked. "Are you up to coming out for breakfast or would you like us to bring it to you? Or are you perhaps still feeling a bit under the weather?"

"What do you eat here? I usually just skip breakfast or have a scrambled egg on buttered toast. I seem to be hungrier than usual though."

"Must have been that journey," Lester said.

Jane nodded in acceptance of the possibility. "I think I'll come out," she said. "If perhaps I could have a few moments to freshen up?"

"Of course."

"I'll show her where to wash," Misty offered.

"Good girl," Peter said, getting up and summoning the others to leave the girls in privacy. He kept Charlie in his arms. After all, how many more times would he be able to hold this little one in his grasp? The answer eluded him.

At seeing the spread, Peter's own eyes became wide. "Bryson, this looks fantastic," Peter said.

"Hey, I helped," Simon said.

"Did you?" Peter asked, genuinely surprised.

"So did I," Timothy declared.

"Did not," Lester said, his arms folded in the usual manner.

"Did so!"

"All right, all right. Let's not worry about it." Peter knew Lester's words could be trusted and that Timothy's words seldom held complete accuracy. He also knew Timothy always sought a way out of clean-up duty, and helping to prepare the meal was one such way. Peter decided not to mention any of that, though. Keep the peace—that was Peter's goal. At least long enough for Jane to like them all. "Thanks to everyone who may have helped."

"Or may not have helped," Lester said under his breath, leaving the conversation and sitting down in front of the table.

"Bryson and me made breakfast by ourselves," Simon said.

"And me!" Timothy added.

Opting to let it go, Peter set Charlie down on one bench, sat across from him, and began to dish up their food.

"Shouldn't we wait for the ladies?" Bryson asked, his dark curls dancing as he finished placing a bowl of eggs on the table. "Or we could start. Whatever you want, Peter." His light brown skin matched the wooden bowl, and his penetrating green eyes seemed to have a power of their own.

"I suppose you're right," Peter said, lifting Charlie's plate and sliding the mango chunks back into another wooden bowl with their counterparts.

"I don't mind," Charlie said in his bold voice. "Can she sit by me?"

"Are you talking about Jane or Misty?" Lester asked. "There are two girls now."

"Will Jane have to wear a disguise too, Peter?" Frank asked. He sported his usual: pinstriped suit, black tie around the neck of what was once a white shirt, and a mobster-style hat. This kid remained true to his fashion sense. The Tally Man always gave a look of annoyance when Frank requested another suit or when he complained. "Those aren't pinstripes!"

he had yelled once. Peter urged him to be quiet, knowing their need for the alliance with the Tally Man. "But Peter," he persisted, only quieter. "Those are polka dots." Peter laughed at the memory.

"What are you laughing about?" Charlie asked.

"Only the Tally Man bringing Frank a polka-dotted suit."

The older Lost Boys erupted with laughter, pointing at Frank and strutting in a mocking way as if wearing a suit.

Charlie stared blankly at everyone. "I don't remember," he said.

At one point, Peter had grown accustomed to not thinking about time at all, but recently, his trips to the Mother Land had forced that concept back into his mind, made it a part of his consciousness again. Peter thought about it. "No, of course not. You hadn't arrived in Neverland yet."

Looking as though this notion puzzled him, as if he'd always been in Neverland, Charlie continued to stare at his guardian.

"Ah, here they come," Peter said. Jane and Misty walked into the center of Hollow Tree Wood where the table and a hungry entourage waited.

"Sit by me!" Charlie yelled.

"And who are you?" Jane asked, taking a seat next to him.

"My name is Charles Michael Williams." His voice sounded the same as it had when he'd first come. The same way it would sound forever if he elected to stay in Neverland. His vocabulary would increase, but the baby-ish tone would always remain.

"Well, isn't that a sophisticated name?" Jane asked.

"What's s—phiscated?" Charlie stuttered.

"It means you're a pansy!" Timothy called from the other end of the table, where Simon and Misty were taking their seats as well. Everyone else had filled in the seats also, Bryson being the last to sit down.

Jane leaned toward Charlie's ear and whispered, "He doesn't know a thing about sophistication. All I meant is that you seem very bright for one so young."

This satisfied Charlie, whose attention turned toward the meal. "Can we start eating now?"

"But I haven't met everyone yet," Jane protested. "It would be weird to eat at a table with a bunch of strangers."

"Ah, do we have to?" Simon asked. "I'm starving."

His sister threw an elbow into his ribs.

"You're not starving," Lester said. "It's impossible to starve in Neverland."

"Is that true?" Jane asked, turning to Peter with inquisitive eyes.

He nodded, finishing a sip of the apple juice in front of him. "Sort of. You certainly don't need as much food. I'm always hungriest when I get back from Earth."

"Fascinating." Jane's eyes stared off in a moment of reflection, as if trying to make sense of this. This intrigued Peter, how she wanted to know about Neverland—her questions and thoughtful responses. It was fitting that someone so interested would take his place. She would probably love to see all his research.

"Well, I'm Lester. Can I eat now?"

"Okay, this is how we'll do it," Peter announced. "Tell Jane your name, age, and what you consider your greatest personal skill or asset."

Timothy and Simon moaned at this request. The others seemed to be working on their responses.

"I'll go," Misty called. "My name is Misty, and I'm eight. My greatest personal asset, whatever that is, is that I'm a girl." Such pride in her feminine voice.

Peter loved having a girl among the Lost Boys. Even after her arrival, they remained the Lost "Boys" since keeping her a secret necessitated a disguise when they traveled, and if the mermaids or the pirates knew a girl lived among them, she would be in danger.

"That's not an asset," her brother said. "That's just annoying."

She elbowed him again.

"Ow!" Simon stood up. "I'm Simon, and I'm also eight. My greatest skill is hunting." He pounded on his chest for affect.

"Whatever, Simon. Last time you caught anything it was a furry black thing with white stripes and strongly smelled of . . . SKUNK! Ring a bell? None of us wanted to eat anything after that." Lester finished his insult and went straight into his introduction. "I'm Lester, fourteen, and my greatest asset is my age. I'm the oldest here, besides you and Peter of course. Oh, and I'm leaving Neverland soon."

Charlie immediately buried his head in his arm and began to cry. His vocabulary kept increasing, but not his emotional stability. That would always remain the same, along with the baby voice.

"That's okay, Charlie." Peter tried in vain to comfort the boy as he watched Jane's reaction. She put an arm around Charlie while looking to Peter and the others.

"Why is Lester leaving Neverland?" Jane asked the group.

Some of them looked to Peter, but nobody spoke. In solemnity, they all sat pondering the "future"—something they usually didn't worry about in Neverland. But with Lester's departure on the horizon, the future was very much present. Watching all their faces, Peter reflected on how much more difficult it would be on them when he left—he who had been here longer than any, greeted them all upon their arrival, and taken care of them. The thought of leaving them filled him with remorse. No, not remorse. Anguish. Not for him, but for them.

He had to say something before this mood overtook them. Low spirits could bring a swarm of gloomy Never fairies. "Misery loves company"— one of the many sayings originating from Neverland.

"He's ready to. That's all. Let's keep going, who's next?"

Jane stared at Peter, as if seeking an answer he wasn't ready to give. He fully expected that she'd ask him about it later. Such a curious thing.

"I'm Bryson." His voice sounded a little dejected still. "I'm eleven, and I'm the best at cooking. Without me, these guys would eat nothing but raw meat and insects."

"Hey, I'm the one who lights the fires," Lester said. "You can't cook meat without a fire."

"Yes you can. You could use a stove," Timothy said.

"Well we don't have one of those, do we?" Lester smacked him upside the head.

Rubbing the sore spot just inflicted by Lester, Timothy stood. "I'm Timothy, I'm nine, and my greatest personal asset is that I fart a lot."

Peter smoothed his eyebrows, then said to Jane, "I would apologize for him, but I don't really see the point. It's best to just expect it."

Jane laughed. "Well I've heard it's extremely healthy. Good for you, Timothy."

"I'm Frank N. Stein," Frank said, ignoring those snickering about Timothy's greatest asset. "I'm nine, and I'm a genius."

Jane burst into a laugh. "Oh, I get it. Frank N. Stein? Like Frankenstein? You can't fool me. What's your real name?"

Frank stared back at Jane. Of all the Lost Boys, Frank showed the least emotion.

"That really is his name." Peter thought to break the news gently, but he couldn't help laughing at the mistake.

"Are you serious?" Jane asked.

"The 'N' stands for Nathaniel," Bryson said.

Jane covered her mouth, but that didn't stop her from making her apologies. "Oh my gosh, Frank. I'm so sorry. I didn't mean to make fun of your name."

"Yeah, I get that a lot."

"No you don't," Lester said. "You hardly ever have the chance to meet someone."

"It *is* a funny name," Preston said, mostly to himself. This start gave him just enough courage to keep talking. "I'm Preston. I'm nine."

They all waited in case he said more, which he didn't.

"What's your greatest asset?" Peter asked.

"I don't know." He shrugged. "I'm smart, I guess."

"I'm Charlie. I'm five. And I run the fastest."

"Well, I can't wait to see that," Jane said.

"I could show you right now!"

"That won't be necessary," Peter said, holding his hand out to discourage Charlie. Peter noticed that everyone had introduced themselves, but something seemed out of place. Finally, it dawned on him. "Where's Karl?"

"One of the chickens decided to wander, and he went to chase it," Charlie said.

"Well, let's not wait for that. Go ahead and eat," Peter said.

"Wait a minute," Bryson urged. "Jane hasn't gone yet."

"That's all right. There's not much you need to know about me."

"Of course, you must go, Jane. It's only fair," Peter said.

"Okay. I'm Jane."

Peter focused on her huge smile. She basked in the attention.

"I'm seventeen." She began considering the other question. "Let's see, I don't cook. Sorry, Bryson. I'm not a genius, and I don't hunt. This is tough."

"Well what's the most interesting thing that ever happened to you?" Lester asked. "Is that good enough, Peter? The eggs are cold now."

"I suppose that will do."

"Oh, that's easy," Jane said. "The most interesting thing that ever happened to me just happened." She looked around at them all and finally settled on Charlie. "I woke up in a tree." She spoke the words as though the experience had been the most amazing thing in the world.

"That's not interesting," Charlie said. "We always do that."

Jane shrugged. "Sorry, that's all I got."

"Let's eat." Timothy began grabbing for food, and the others followed until the whole table abounded in commotion and the happy slapping of lips at mealtime.

Peter watched Jane, who only watched the others and helped Charlie now and then with something. She finally looked at Peter. "You still hungry?" he asked.

"It's a little too boisterous for me. I'm getting a kick out of this. You?"

"I'm not so hungry anymore." He couldn't say where his appetite had gone, but watching Jane interact with the Lost Boys seemed to be about all he needed at the moment.

"What about you?" she asked. "How old are you? What's your greatest personal skill or asset?" Their conversation continued, seemingly unnoticed by the others, except perhaps by Lester and Preston, who always listened, even when nothing was being said.

"I'm seventeen too. Almost eighteen actually." His lips straightened at the thought. It was the reason the pirates sought to do him harm.

"How'd you get so old?"

He shrugged. "Couldn't stop going back to Earth. And let's see, my greatest personal skill or asset—" He thought for a moment. "Patience."

"Good one," she said.

What he didn't tell her then was that he'd been patient for too long—decades, long enough to carry past a century—and his patience, like the time on his age dial, was running out.

BUTTERFLIES AND LULLABIES

*P*eter watched Jane as she helped with the cleanup. Dressed in form-fitting jeans and a wool sweater, she looked overheated. With her sleeves rolled up, she plunged her hands into the soapy water as she and Bryson laughed together. Charlie tugged at the bottom of her sweater, leaving a bit of dirt behind.

"What is it, little one?"

Peter marveled at Neverland Jane. Once brash and edgy, she now resembled a saint more than a teenager. Perhaps caring for children really was her niche, and when in that role all the prickles melted away. He didn't dare hope her attitude toward him had changed and fully expected the sass to return eventually. But for now, he found watching her a pleasant pastime.

"Will you come play with me?" Charlie asked Jane.

"Of course I will," Jane said, smiling down at him and shaking the water off her hands.

"No, no, Charlie. You know the rules. School first," Peter said, ever vigilant about ensuring at least some observation and study.

Jane wiped her forehead and placed her hands on her hips as she turned to Peter. "You have a school? Isn't the point of Neverland to avoid things like that?"

"Don't let his pouty face fool you. We take a relaxed approach to school here."

"Can we go to the Never heated pools?" Simon asked.

"That sounds like the perfect way to show Jane how we do school around here," Peter said.

"Aw, that means I have to put regular clothes on," Frank said.

"If you want to do any sliding, yes," Peter said. "We don't need to be asking the Tally Man for any suits right now."

"Yay! We're going to the Never heated pools! Yay, yay, yay, yay, yay!" Little Charlie jumped around in the joyous, energetic way that only a young boy can.

"Sliding? That doesn't sound educational. And Never heated pools? Is that where you bathe?"

An uproarious laughter echoed from every Lost Boy, and even Misty. "We don't bathe," Timothy said.

"Speak for yourself," Lester said, eyeing Timothy up and down. "Some of us bathe."

"Yes, but not in the Never heated pools," Misty pointed out, still laughing some.

Jane came close to Peter, and in that moment, he felt she trusted him. This inkling gave him mixed emotions. His plan depended on earning her trust. He couldn't shake the idea, however, that his plan was more of a scheme. Guilt won over for a moment as she came close enough that the fibers of her wool sweater brushed against his mostly bare arm.

"What are the Never heated pools then?" Jane asked.

Peter clapped his hands. "You shall see," he said only to Jane. He then called out instructions to the others, making sure they finished cleaning Hollow Wood and brought their school supplies.

"Will I need anything?" Jane asked.

"I have an extra sketchbook you can have," Peter said.

With the excitement of their destination in mind, the Lost Boys prepared instantly, and they all ventured through the wood, sketchbooks and writing utensils in hand. Charlie rode on Jane's back. Watching the Lost Boys with Jane as they tromped through the surrounding trees, Peter felt he could almost sneak away now. He forced this idea out of his head.

Lester fell back for a moment. "Peter? How long before you go?"

The question jolted Peter, especially given the thoughts so recently on his mind.

Lester noticed his concern. "You don't have to tell me if you don't want to."

"Tell you what?" asked Preston. Ever the observer, he had sneaked up on them from behind.

Peter gave Lester a reassuring smile before looking back to Preston. "Oh, nothing. Nothing to worry about. Let's hurry, shall we? The others are getting ahead."

"All right," Preston said, hanging his head a little.

Peter hated to disappoint, knowing how much Preston valued being a part of whatever conversation took place. He also knew it would all be forgotten in a flicker.

"I saw a fairy!" Jane's exclamation could be heard even from a distance.

"Where?" Simon asked.

"What color was it?" Misty asked.

"It went that way." Jane pointed and took off in pursuit. The Lost Boys joined her search, and Peter followed as well, eager to witness this first encounter. It never wore off—the potent memory of seeing a Never fairy for the first time. Not for Peter, at least. The first fairy he ever saw had been the color of grapefruit.

"I think it's green," Jane called.

Green. So many options. It could be lime green, sage green, forest green. It could be jealous, greedy, nervous. So many green possibilities.

"There it is." Her excitement waned. "Oh, no. I don't think it's a fairy after all."

"That's a butterfly, silly," Charlie said.

Peter caught up with the crowd and saw Jane holding out her hand hoping the butterfly would climb aboard. "It's so vibrant." The butterfly obliged and crawled onto an outstretched finger. "And so tiny." She examined it. "Are Never fairies this little?"

"About," Peter said. "Just shaped differently—a little longer and leaner on the wingspan. And they glow, even under the Never sun."

"All right everyone, you've got your specimen. Take out your sketchbooks and draw it." He crouched down to see it up close. "Here, Jane. Let me take it, and you can help Charlie with his drawing."

Peter pinched the butterfly's wings together and lifted it off of Jane's hand. Charlie slid down Jane's back to the ground and flipped open his sketchbook.

Peter inspected the butterfly as he held it out for the Lost Boys to see. Its wings were delicate and a bit slippery, but Peter held firm so that when he let go, the butterfly would still be able to flutter.

"Is this school?" Jane asked.

Peter turned to her. She sat on the long grass of the meadow with Charlie at her side. All the others sat in the grass as well, drawing and writing. They knew their assignment and they did it willingly. Peter nodded in answer to her question and turned back to the butterfly. He sensed it began to feel antsy and would soon take off.

"I love it," Jane said, tilting her head back and looking up to the sky. "Hey, isn't the sun a little high for this time of morning?"

Charlie let out a youthful giggle.

"What?" Jane asked. "What did I say now?"

Peter let the butterfly go. "You're in Neverland now, Jane. There is no morning."

"Hey! I wasn't finished drawing," Misty said.

Jane sat up a little straighter. "What do you mean there is no morning? I woke up and the sun was shining. At least, I thought it was. The rooster crowed." She began to look around at the others, as if seeking for someone to defend her or take her side. "I heard him. We ate eggs."

Bryson shook his head and scoffed.

"Think of the seasons," Peter said, taking advantage of the teaching moment. "If you want it to be winter, you have to travel there."

He waited for her to figure it out and it didn't take long.

"So . . . if you want to sleep, you have to find the night."

"No, you can sleep anywhere. Charlie does it all the time," Timothy said, laughing up a storm. "Last week he slept on top of one of the hens."

"I did not," Charlie said.

Jane thought some more. "Okay, I think I have it. If you want to sleep, you sleep. But if you want it to be night, you have to go there."

"Well done, Jane," Peter said.

She beamed and shrugged her shoulders. "I'm catching on."

Charlie announced the completion of his work, and Jane stood up and ballyhooed the simple drawing until everyone applauded.

"Can we go to the pools now?" Charlie asked.

"Sure. Lester can stay here with those who are finishing, and we'll go give the slides a test run. Make sure they're safe." Peter winked at Charlie, who stood with pride and took Jane by the hand.

"C'mon, Jane. Let's go. Let's go."

Leaving the meadow, Peter led Jane and Charlie along a path through a sparse woodland until they reached the bottom of the hill. A rocky path led to the top, and Peter turned to Jane to witness her seeing the Never heated pools for the first time. Her eyes widened upon seeing the expanse of bubbling pools, which stretched into the distance, almost past the line of sight, surrounded almost entirely by trees.

"Pretty amazing, huh?" Peter asked.

"What is this place?"

"We already told you, Jane. Don't you listen?" Charlie chided, earning a giggle from Jane.

"Wait for us," a voice called.

Peter stepped back to look down the hill to see the rest in tow behind Timothy.

"We'd better hurry if we're going to have the first ride." Peter grabbed Charlie underneath his arms and threw him into the closest pool. Charlie squealed in delight before plunging beneath the water and quickly popping back up. Peter turned to Jane, hit with a sudden urge to lift her and throw her into the water as well.

"Oh, no you don't."

Could she read his mind? "Suit yourself," he said, turning to jump in, but before he even bent his knees, two hands shoved him from behind, catching him off guard. He glanced backward as he fell in, glimpsing Jane's impish smile before he smacked into the muddy pool.

Peter felt the warm water immerse him, blocking out everything else until he resurfaced to hear Jane laughing profusely.

"Now what?" she asked just as the remainder of the party arrived.

Peter turned to Charlie. "Shall we show her?"

"Yeah!"

Peter pulled himself out of the water, and Charlie followed. They walked toward the start of the slide, where the pools overflowed often enough to create a permanently muddy hill. Peter sat at the top, looking down and reminding himself of the course—where to avoid trees and drop-offs—as Charlie plopped down on his lap. A surge of adrenaline rushed through him, and he pushed off. Charlie let out a shriek of delight as they plunged down a steep slant in the hill and curved around a group of trees. The mud slopped and squished beneath him, sending up splashes of thick, wet dirt that splattered their arms, chests and faces. Before reaching the end of the course, they abruptly landed in a pool that stood in the middle of the muddy path.

"Looks like this will be the end of the road this time, Charlie."

The little boy rolled off Peter's lap and playfully splashed around in the muddy water.

"Watch out!"

Peter turned to see a sliding parade of Lost Boys—Timothy, Frank, and Preston came rushing toward him and Charlie. Timothy slid off to the right, rolling and laughing at each slippery turn. Frank and Preston splashed into the puddle, one on top of the other. Peter often thought of them as triplets. Though they looked nothing alike, they shared the same age. Preston got up first, smiling at the others, his timidity showing even in the midst of their frivolity. He looked toward Peter, a question in his eyes, and Peter could sense that he knew something was coming. The constant guilt coursing throughout Peter's veins was taking a toll. Weary at the thought of facing any of them with his decision, Peter considered leaving as soon as he could. He imagined tiptoeing away just before everyone gathered for their next meal, or perhaps he would try to sneak away from mud sliding earlier than the rest and take off then.

A joyful cry jerked him from his reverie. Jane came speeding down the hill, train style, her arms wrapped around Simon's waist and his arms around his sister. The three bumped down the slippery hill until they thudded in the small pool.

Jane looked up at Peter, her smile gigantic and her wool sweater ruined.

The sight of her even darker mud-streaked hair and sloppy, dripping sweater forced a laugh from Peter. "I should have thought to give you a different shirt. Looks like that one will never be the same again. Sorry," Peter said, smiling ruefully.

"*That* was worth it." Breathless, Jane helped the others out of the pool, splashing everyone in the process. Intentionally. Watching her, Peter thought of how, if he left now, he would never understand her: why she had even considered coming with him (aside from the fact that he had tricked her and weakened her defenses with fairy dust) and what she was running away from in the first place. He wondered what her famous parents might have to do with any of it and whether they missed her. A twinge of sadness pierced him.

"Look out below!" Bryson came rushing toward them, his large body threatening to crash into any one of them or perhaps even all of them. Peter and Jane both reached toward Charlie, making sure he stayed away from Bryson's line of travel. Not that it would have mattered much— Neverland's gravitational pull dimmed in comparison to Earth's.

Karl appeared at the top of the hill. Peter never wondered where the boy roamed. Karl enjoyed being alone and free, living his life one adventure after another. He began sliding down the hill on his feet, careful not to fall down until he grabbed hold of a vine and swung toward them. The Lost Boys let out a cheer of encouragement. He whizzed past them until the pendulum pulled him back again in the other direction. This time he dropped into the pool, miraculously landing on his feet. He held his hands up for a moment and then took a bow.

"Jane, this is Karl."

Karl whipped around to see her, his wet hair slapping his face and sticking to it in the process. He appeared to blush at having a female guest he'd been unaware of. Peter had never seen the likes from Karl. Then again, who knew when any of them had last seen a girl other than Misty? Unless you counted the mermaids. And Peter didn't.

Karl giggled pathetically, words gone and any attempt at a greeting eluding him.

"Hi, Karl. It's good to finally meet you," Jane said.

"Last one to the top's a rotten egg," Karl called, taking off toward the rocky staircase that would lead them back to the top.

Charlie begged Bryson for a piggyback ride when Jane pronounced she needed to take a breather before going again. Bryson gave in as always, leaving Peter and Jane alone.

Peter glanced up to the top of the hill where Lester looked down at them. "Aren't you coming?" Peter called.

Lester cupped his hands around his mouth and shouted, "I'll stay up here."

"Extraordinary," Peter whispered.

"What is?"

Peter looked toward Jane, taken with her interest and endless curiosity. "Lester has never turned down mud sliding before." He considered for a moment what this truly meant. "I think it's time."

"Time for what?" She took a step toward Peter.

"Time for him to leave Neverland."

"Why would anyone want to leave this place?" She gazed up at Lester, as if truly puzzled by the revelation that he might leave. "I want to stay forever."

"Are you sure that isn't the fairy dust talking?" Peter grinned at her.

Her stern gaze told Peter she hadn't caught on to his teasing yet. He couldn't blame her. He hadn't teased anyone in ages, except for maybe a pirate here and there.

Finally she understood and broke into a smile. "You haven't slipped me any more of that, have you?"

Peter bowed his head, almost ashamed of how he'd used it against her. Almost, but not quite. Things seemed to be turning out better than he ever could have engineered.

"Here they come," Jane said. She grabbed hold of his arm and pulled him farther from the path. They found a large rock to sit on and watched the children go down again and again.

Finally, after several turns, Charlie came and climbed onto Jane's lap while the others ran back up the stairs for another trip down the mud slide.

"I'm tired."

"Oh," Jane said, accepting him into the cradle of her arms. She looked to Peter for an explanation, but he only shrugged.

With eyes closed, Charlie asked Jane if she knew any lullabies. He snuggled his head into the crook of her elbow.

"Lullabies? I could probably conjure one. I was raised by a British nanny, you know."

"Were you?" Peter asked, surprised by this bit of information.

She glanced at Peter before answering. "Yes. What's so surprising about that?"

Peter shook his head. "Oh, nothing. I just remembered how you introduced yourself as Mary Poppins that day at the train station."

She smiled in answer. "Well, she was no Mary Poppins, but I loved her just the same." She looked down at Charlie who appeared to be drifting. "I do remember one song she used to sing."

Jane opened her mouth and began to sing, a bit shaky at first, but growing stronger until her voice arrested Peter's mind, nearly putting him in a trance.

"Daylight scatters all around. Darkness gathers in its place. The moon shines down from above. Starlight sprinkles its love and kisses your face. And I am staying by your side until dreamland pulls you through. I'll not let the shadows pierce, nor nightmares so fierce—frighten you. Frighten you. And when you dream, I'll be there too."

She looked at Peter as she began the second verse. "Hand in hand we'll touch the sky. Flying over oceans deep. We'll leave behind a dusting trail, as through the glowing clouds we sail, our dreams to keep."

Peter knew why she'd looked at him. The song described a moment they'd shared together. She looked away now, focusing on the children. He closed his eyes and allowed her angelic voice to enfold him. "Then landing back inside your room, I'll tuck you into bed once more. You'll close your eyes and count to five. Then the morning sun will rise and light the shore. Light the shore. And when you wake, I'll be there too. I'll be here too."

The music died, and Peter opened his eyes once more. Mesmerized, he found it difficult to stop gaping at her, even though the silence stretched. Charlie let out a loud, unflattering snore, giving them all permission to speak again.

"You're a singer." Peter said it as if it meant something profound, like maybe she didn't belong here after all. Perhaps she'd been running away from the doldrums of her daily routine and heading for a life of fame and fortune all her own. She'd never find that in Neverland.

"Oh, it's nothing." She swayed her head away from him for a moment. "Well, I did sing quite a bit as a child. I took lessons from one of the greats. Competed. Even won sometimes."

Peter couldn't take the suspense. This made him nervous somehow. He thought that her running away, leaving school, meant she would be desperate for a place to stay, for people she could love and who loved her in return. But she had sincere, authentic talent. "Is that what you planned to do after running away?" He spoke quietly, not wanting Charlie to hear or even remotely remember any part of this conversation.

She shrugged. "I guess. I know several agents that would probably work with me. I even did a cover song for a record company once."

Peter only stared.

"What?" Jane asked.

He shook his head. "Nothing. It's just that you're full of surprises. That's all." In reality, he feared that for all her enthusiasm for Neverland, she didn't really need it. Or any of them.

"Fine, if you don't want to tell me."

"Tell you what?"

"Whatever it is you're keeping from me. Your thoughts that don't make it past your tongue." She leaned closer to him, and he found his eyes couldn't help but look at her lips. "But you know what happens to words that go unspoken?" she whispered. "You choke on them."

Still supporting Charlie, she scooted off the rock and began descending the hill. Peter watched her try not to slip, musing about how there was much more to Jane than he had noticed before. Outward appearances could be so deceiving. Perhaps he'd have to slip her some more fairy dust after all. Or tell her the truth. Regardless of the exact method he would use, he still saw her as his only way out.

FAREWELL FIRE

*P*eter watched Jane interact with Karl as they did the dishes side by side, having both lost at drawing straws to earn such an honor. She seemed at ease, joyful even. After his interaction with Jane at the mud slide, Peter thought she would diminish somehow, seem more on guard. Her free spirit soared higher than ever, though. She let out a ring of laughter at something Karl said, her arms immersed in bubbles.

Lester encroached on Peter's pondering. "It's time, Peter," he said. "I can feel it. I'm ready to leave."

"I know," Peter said in return, sipping his cup of Never ginger tea. "I can see it." Peter looked at Lester, who sat beside him on a bench made from Neverland Pointed trees—one of the only ones they'd ever cut down for wood. Wanting Lester's opinion before he left, he asked, "What do you think of Jane?"

"What do you mean?"

"How do you think she would fare here? If you and I both left?"

"She's brilliant. The Lost Boys love her, and Misty. She's charming and funny and a bit wild. Perfect for Neverland. Why? And why are you avoiding the topic of me leaving?"

Peter smiled at him. Nothing got past Lester.

"Lester's leaving?" Preston asked. Peter knew better than to be surprised that the boy had overheard. He probably wasn't even eavesdropping. That kid could hear across the whole of Hollow Tree Wood. Peter also knew better than to be surprised that this seemed to be news to Preston again. Neverland possessed a powerful forgetfulness, but Peter had never been able to research the potency, regularity, or triggering factors of the forgetfulness and knew little about it, only that it was a possibility.

Peter gave Preston a reassuring smile before leaning closer to Lester. "I wasn't avoiding the topic. Not really. In fact, if you'll go and pack your belongings, I'll fetch some fairy dust, and we can head out to Winter Quarter as soon as things are cleaned up. It wouldn't be a proper good-bye without a fire. And it wouldn't be a proper fire without a bit of darkness. If we're still in a purple moon, I think that will ensure you good luck for your journey."

Lester's face lit up.

"I know you'll be fine down there. Or is it up? I always forget," Peter said.

Lester laughed a bit, but also rolled his eyes, cuing Peter to the fact that Lester didn't think his joke funny.

"I'll let you tell everyone what the celebration is all about."

Lester's brow crinkled in worry. "Me?"

"Yes, you. If you're going to leave, you get to be the one to tell everyone." Peter doubted he'd be strong enough to swallow his own prescription when the time came. Would he be able to tell everyone, or would he sneak off without a good-bye? How long would it take before they all forgot him? But Peter remembered other Lost Boys that had traveled back to the Mother Land. Maybe they would remember. Lester's plans to leave had come up a few times, but each time felt like the first: Charlie would burst into tears, and all the Lost Boys seemed even more lost. Until they forgot again. But Peter hadn't told anyone but Lester about his own plans to leave. It would be a total shock at first, maybe even devastating. Perhaps forgetting would be better. This thought both comforted him and filled him with an overpowering sadness.

He longed for the opportunity to speak with Jane alone; it seemed impossible with so many children needing attention or feeling nosy. He'd been considering simply telling her the truth, but he also wanted to learn a bit more about her. As ideal as she seemed, he questioned whether she'd devote her life to this place so readily regardless of his openness.

Lester stood next to him and cleared his throat. "Everyone, I have an announcement. After we're finished cleaning up, we'll be packing for a trip to Winter Quarter. We'll have a fire, and afterward, I'll be going back to the Mother Land."

Peter looked to Jane first. Her hands dripped over the water basin, suspended in stillness, and she wore a puzzled expression on her face.

Charlie began to cry, and Simon and Misty looked so forlorn. Karl dried his hands and ran into the wood. He probably wouldn't reappear before they left, given his gift for the enjoyment of solitude. Lester took a deep breath and retreated to his tree, presumably to pack what few possessions he'd be taking with him.

Jane approached Peter after looking to see that Misty had stepped in to comfort Charlie. She sat next to him on the bench, leaning in so close Peter could smell the lingering scent of the sweet soap she'd chosen for her bath after mud sliding. She looked him squarely in the eye, as if forbidding him to tell anything but the whole and exact truth.

Peter attempted to swallow the nervousness away. She'd never looked at him like that before. How could she be demanding with a simple facial expression?

"What does it mean, Peter?"

"It means he's going back to Earth." Peter watched her eyes as she absorbed his words. "For good."

Jane nodded slightly. "You mean, he won't be coming back?"

"He's decided to grow up."

Only then did she look away from him, her eyes peering down to the dirt on the ground while she used her hands to brace herself on the splintery wood.

Peter looked around to see that everyone had disappeared, leaving them alone. He opened his mouth, trying to remember what he'd planned to ask her when they were alone, but Jane spoke first.

"How is it that you're so grown, Peter? I vaguely remember asking you that before, when we met at the train station. Aren't you supposed to be a little boy?"

Truth. He'd have to answer her questions truthfully if he had any hope of escaping this place. He could sense she was onto his scheme in some measure, or at least that she could tell when he kept things from her.

"I age every time I go to Earth." Peter drank the last of his tea, sipping out each tiny droplet. He placed his teacup on the ground and interlaced his hands, resting his arms on his knees as he leaned forward. "Aging came gradually at first. I went back infrequently after first coming here." He turned to her. "But recently I've gone more and more, staying longer and longer. We don't count time in Neverland—there really isn't any purpose—but I've been to Earth enough over several decades to almost reach adulthood."

The Lost Boys began coming out of their trees. Charlie ran to Jane, jumping into her ready arms and planting his wet face onto her shoulder.

"Hey. Don't cry, little guy. Lester's just going on an adventure. We need to be happy for him."

Peter watched Jane get up. She held Charlie close and swayed back and forth in her sleek boots. She wore an old shirt of Peter's and the only pair of jeans she'd brought with her. They hugged her legs slightly, and the shirt came almost to her knees.

"Will they need warmer clothing?" she asked, pulling Peter's attention back to her face.

"Um, no." He rubbed a hand through his hair and chided himself. Had he really just been noticing her figure?

"But aren't we going to the Winter Quarter?"

Peter cleared his throat, somehow fearing his voice would crack if he spoke again. He tested for a moment. "Um . . ." It seemed to be good. "We'll be flying so we won't need any clothes."

"This is new," Jane said, turning away from him. "Did you hear that, Charlie? Peter says we don't need any clothes at all."

Peter could feel the heat erupt in his face. How could something be so benign in his head and come out sounding so scandalous? Ashamed at his fumble and perplexed by her forward interpretation, Peter quickly got up and left. Even after reaching his hollow tree and closing the door he could feel the heat throughout his entire body. The solitude did little to comfort him, so he busied himself with securing enough fairy dust to get them all there and back, and a little extra for Lester just in case he ever wanted to return.

A knock on the door filled him with dread. Would it be Jane asking for a more clarified explanation? Better get it over with. Peter opened the door to Bryson—a welcome sight indeed. Peter let out the air he'd been holding captive. "What is it, Bryson?"

"I packed snacks for everyone."

"Great. Thank you, Bryson. We'd all starve without you, I'm sure."

"Peter, we're almost out of food."

"Right." Peter still struggled to get his blunder with Jane out of his head. "Well, hopefully the Tally Man will come soon. He'll be bringing some things. In the meantime, we can cut down the number of eggs we use, to ration a bit. Let's also plan a trip to Summer Quarter for some more vegetables."

"But Peter, what about the pirates?"

Peter put a hand on Bryson's shoulder. "Not to worry, my friend. We'll be careful. I think they're still on Earth anyway." At least, that's what Peter hoped. He was fairly certain he hadn't reached eighteen yet but needed to steer clear of them just in case.

Peter exited his tree, letting Bryson go to finish his preparations. Jane still held Charlie on her hip. Peter approached her, a spark of bravery helping him overcome his previous fright. "I can guarantee you'll see a fairy soon," he said.

"Really?" she asked, a gleeful smile gracing her face. She turned to Charlie. "Did you hear that? We're going to see a fairy."

"So?" Charlie said. "I've seen fairies thousands of times. No, millions."

"Someone's still upset," Jane said, giving Peter a brave smile.

"And you? How do you feel about Lester leaving, Jane?"

"I'm not sure. But I'll keep you posted on any developments."

Peter smiled at her. "Sounds good." Now or never. Everyone would be ready and gathered soon, except maybe Karl. "I'm sorry about what I said before. That's not what I meant."

"What?" she said, sounding clueless.

He couldn't bear saying it again and risking the embarrassment. "There is no need for coats and gloves in Winter Quarter. Not even a jacket. Well, unless you go there on foot."

"What do you mean?" Jane asked. Charlie finally slipped out of her arms and ran off as if he had no thought of Lester at all.

"We'll be flying which means we'll be using fairy dust. Fairy dust protects from changes in temperature, allowing your body to regulate its preferred temperature precisely, no matter what the weather."

"Are you serious?" Jane asked.

"Of course."

"That's . . . awesome." Her smile lit up the entire clearing. "I've been itching to fly again."

"Have you?" This both surprised Peter and thrilled him, although he could not say why on either account. "Let's go then."

Lester gathered the others, and Peter began handing out the fairy dust, taking a pinch from his black pouch and giving a measure to everyone.

As the children began to lift off the ground, Jane stepped close to Peter. "Are they going to be all right? What about Charlie? Does he need any help?"

Her questions amused Peter, and he couldn't hold back his laughter. "You're nervous, aren't you?"

"No, I'm . . ."

"It's okay. For some reason, the second time is more nerve-racking than the first. You wonder if it will be as exciting or if it will be even more terrifying. At least, that's how it was for me."

"You remember your second time flying?"

"Yes, clearly."

"But I thought you had a poor memory."

Peter stared at her. "Well, yes. Neverland does that to you. But I remember the first and second time. And I remember flying with you. Actually, all the time I've spent on Earth has brought back quite a bit."

"Hey, are you two comin'?" Timothy shouted from far above them.

"Oh my goodness, I am nervous. I'm downright scared. They're so high up there."

She might not have been aware of Peter's plans yet, but she acted like a mother already. Peter dropped a pinch of fairy dust on her head and took off, leaving her to find her own way this time. He turned to watch her lift off the ground, unsure and wobbly at first but growing in confidence and skill, although she never did quite catch up to them. Nobody seemed keen on staying behind to escort her either. They all probably sought to show off a bit, including Peter.

Flying over Winter Quarter, Peter marveled at the beauty. The light purple moon lit the sky only slightly, but the reflection on the snow below made the trees visible enough. He never tired of the beauty of Neverland.

In some respects, Earth's wonders paled in comparison. He would miss it all, especially the flying.

Peter followed Lester and the others as they landed in a clearing where a fire already blazed. Karl stood nearby, his face lit up by the flame. Tricky little devil.

Lester slapped Karl's back and thanked him. Tender emotions filled Peter, and he wanted nothing more than to get it over with, not only Lester's good-bye but his own. He couldn't leave now, though. He'd have to wait a bit to let the pain of Lester's good-bye dull some. Then again, maybe it would be better to leave together. No, Peter still had a few things to do before he went. Lester could go now, and Peter envied him.

Jane finally landed beside him. "Thanks for the help back there," she said.

Peter smiled at the sound of her voice and her sarcasm. "I knew you'd be all right. How was it?"

"Amazing." She elbowed him then joined the others around the fire, her feet crunching in the icy snow.

Peter stood apart watching them all, knowing they'd want to savor this artificial piece of time when all he wanted was to rush through it. Neverland only experienced change as people came and went, and there'd been so much of that lately, it was almost as if time existed. Perhaps that simply came from going to Earth so often recently, but Peter felt as though he was counting down to something. Time slipped through the unsuspecting pockets of the Earth, while on Neverland it floated through the air like mist that would never dissipate. Peter couldn't decide which he preferred.

These thoughts came to an abrupt halt when Charlie asked Jane if she knew any good-bye songs. Peter didn't think he could bear to hear her sing again. Not now. Emotion choked him at the thought. Luckily, Jane broke into a mocking little ditty that he guessed was meant to break the somber mood. She even galloped around the fire once or twice, and Peter loved her for it. Everyone laughed instead of producing the tears that probably threatened them all.

"How about some good-bye jokes?" Timothy asked. "I could tell one. What did the chicken say before he crossed the road?"

"What?" Charlie asked.

"Good-BOK!" He laughed out loud, and Charlie followed suit. Frank let Timothy know how much his joke stank, and almost everyone else agreed. Even Peter. Jane seemed to be the only one (other than Charlie) who genuinely found it humorous. Peter couldn't seem to tear his gaze away from her. She simply beamed in Peter's eyes, almost commanding his attention.

"I'd like to say something," Lester began.

Peter's heart fell as he realized where this would lead. Lester had been his rock for so long that Peter couldn't even remember how he had coped before Lester came. Peter's thoughts ran about, playing memories like little blinking still frames in his mind. He thought about their flight to Winter Quarter and how, other than the flight back to Earth, it would be Lester's last. He'd already had his last mud slide, his last meal made by the talented Bryson, his last swim in the Never heated pools, and his last time in charge when Peter had gone to get Jane.

"Are you okay?" Jane stood next to him, trying to make eye contact, but Peter couldn't bring himself to look her in the eye. Not now. "Hey, look at me."

Peter shook his head. A tear hung from his lashes, and he didn't want her to see.

"To Peter." Lester held up his hand as if it held a glass and everyone clanged imaginary glasses all around them. Peter had missed the entire speech.

"Perhaps if you said a few words," Jane whispered to him, probably encouraging him to pull out of his depressing thoughts.

Summoning courage from somewhere, Peter cleared his throat and began. "Lester, from the moment you revealed to me your plans of returning to the Mother Land, I knew you'd made the right choice. No one could do better. You've been a help and a protector to the Lost Boys."

"Hey," Misty said.

"And Misty," Peter added. He held his own hand up now, as if cupping a glass.

"Thank you," Misty said.

"To be frank, Lester, I don't know what we will do without you." That stupid tear fell down Peter's cheek, despite his demands. "To Lester."

Everyone raised another imaginary glass and toasted their dear friend.

"I know it is difficult for many of you to understand why Lester is leaving. But there comes a time in every Lost Boy's heart, when the decision is made to grow up. Not growing up is fun at first. And there is much to learn without getting any older. But some things, some experiences, would be lost forever, if . . ." Peter fought hard not to look at Jane. His mind blanked, the forgetfulness of Neverland taking hold. The one thing Peter knew in that moment was that he was giving his reasons, not Lester's. "Lester is ready to grow up. Neverland is not providing the progress that he craves. There is no shame in growing up. No sorrow."

"I'll never grow up!" Charlie yelled, folding his arms across his chest and contorting his lips into a pronounced pout.

"Perhaps, Charlie," Peter said. "But tonight, Lester is."

"Here, here," Karl said, raising his imaginary glass. Lester beamed.

Jane locked her arm with Peter's, and the gesture gave him just enough strength to pull it together.

"That was perfect," she whispered. "Great job."

"Thank you," Peter whispered back. "For the compliment. And for the arm. I hadn't realized how much I needed a little support."

She squeezed his arm gently before letting go to pick up Charlie, who appeared to be only a breath or two from falling asleep despite his recent protest and tantrum.

Bryson passed around the snacks, but Peter couldn't eat. He followed Jane around as she spoke with Lester about his plans and then as she conversed with Karl about whether he thought he'd ever return to Earth or not. Being near her gave him comfort somehow, and he needed the strength. Charlie drooled on Jane's shoulder, sound asleep, and the others played a game of marbles near the fire.

"I'm ready to go," Lester announced, and they all turned toward him, every one of them avoiding looking directly at his face, except Jane.

"Good-bye. Or 'Good-BOK' as the chicken would say," Timothy said.

Peter couldn't bear it any longer. Jane stepped in to give Lester a hug, and Lester kissed Charlie's forehead. Karl turned and walked into the forest, and the other children seemed too timid for a hug or even to utter a word.

"Wish me luck. I'll be thinking of you." With that, Lester lifted into the air and flew out of sight, darting in front of the gentle purple moon for effect.

So many sulky faces. Misty began to cry, and Simon joined in. Preston announced that he was going back to Hollow Tree Wood.

"Are you sure you don't know any good-bye songs?" Misty asked Jane.

"Well, maybe I can think of one." Then, pointing to the sleeping child in her arms, she added, "I'll need someone to take this lump, though, because my back is killing me."

Peter stepped in and retrieved Charlie. He knew the warm mass on his chest would protect him some from runaway emotions. He'd need the distraction once Jane began to sing. Luckily the tune that came from her lips held a certain joviality rather than the typical glumness of good-bye songs.

"Good-bye, good-bye, my friend. I hope to see you again. Good-bye, good-bye, my friend. I hate to see this end. Good-bye, good-bye for now. Let's give a smile somehow. Good-bye, good-bye for now. No need to wear that frown."

As Jane sang, a horde of fairies approached, all glowing a pinkish-purple for curiosity. Jane smiled wide at the sight, but she did not let that divert her from the song.

"By and by you'll see, that this was meant to be. By and by you'll see, that you are livin' free. By and by the time will come and ease your mind. By and by the time will come and ease your mind."

The song helped to provide Peter some comfort, as did Charlie's peaceful presence. Although, perhaps not the drool.

"Good-bye, good-bye my friend. I hope to see you again. Good-bye, good-bye for now. Let's give a smile somehow."

Jane finished the song, and almost instantly the fairies began to change color: some turned the color of mud for confusion and others, back to whatever color they'd most likely been before the lure of the music had pulled them in. Jane watched them for a moment until most were out of sight. "Who's ready to go back to Spring Quarter?" Jane asked. "It won't be so dark. That might make us all feel better."

Peter doubted anything could make him feel better. Why in the universe did he feel so overcome with grief?

PREPARATIONS

*N*ormalcy. Peter knew that's what would help everyone move forward, even if the steps were laced with bitterness for a time. Adventure. Movement. Wonder. He had to be strong for the others, and while he missed Lester fiercely, Jane's optimism and perpetual joy kept him going. The children seemed to be forgetting, which helped, but every once in a while, Charlie or Misty would break into tears or ask for Lester. Charlie even asked once if Lester left because of him. It nearly broke Peter's heart. Jane jumped in and cleverly told Charlie that he was the reason it was so hard for Lester to leave.

"It didn't seem hard," Charlie replied. "He couldn't wait to get out of here."

Trying not to laugh, Jane chose to distract him rather than get into an argument.

The need for distractions dimmed, and Neverland life carried on. On and on and on.

Peter also began to prepare for all he had to teach Jane. He gathered his notes and even wrote her a few informational letters. Mostly he would need to show her everything, and that was what he planned to begin immediately. He also felt he owed her a better fairy experience since the last one had been so brief and sorrowful. She'd hardly had the opportunity to enjoy it.

Peter approached Bryson while he made his bed. "Bryson, can we have a word?"

"Sure thing, Peter, just let me get this blanket smoothed out."

Peter smirked at the attempt. Bryson cooked like a professional, but his bed making needed practice. The crooked covers left one corner of the Never straw mattress exposed, and several lumps remained even after the smoothing.

"What is it?" Bryson asked.

Peter spoke directly, knowing he needed Bryson to step up, now that Lester had gone, but he also had every faith in the eleven-year-old. "Bryson, I'd like you to take Lester's place. As my right-hand man and confidant. It will be more responsibility, and I know you already take on plenty. If I need to travel to the Mother Land for any reason, you will oversee the others."

"But what about Karl? He's older."

Peter thought about the question, analyzing his tone. Peter recognized a hint of self-doubt, which he deemed easier to overcome than unwillingness. "Bryson, you are the man for the job. I'm sure of it. You are good with the little ones, calm under pressure—most of the time—and you're the most capable one here."

"Well, what about Jane? Can't she be in charge?"

Peter had failed to predict this question. It lingered in the air like the scent of smoke after a campfire. He couldn't tell Bryson that Jane would be taking Peter's place eventually, and therefore Bryson clearly needed to take Lester's place.

"You're going to have to trust me on this one. Jane has her place here now, to be sure, but I'm asking you to do this, and you alone. Your first task will be to look after the others while I show Jane around Neverland."

Bryson bowed his head in contemplation for a moment, his spry, black ringlets almost mocking Peter with their joviality. Peter hadn't experienced much joy since Lester's departure, but he looked forward to taking Jane and leaving the others behind.

"I'll do it on one condition."

"What's that?" Peter tried not to smile.

"That everyone helps me cook sometimes."

"Are you sure about that? If I remember correctly, you weren't interested in eating the last time somebody else tried cooking."

"Well, maybe I get tired of cooking all the time."

"I'm sure you do, but remember Bryson, we don't actually need to eat here in Neverland. It's more of a habit and a luxury than a necessity."

"Well, that's beside the point, Peter. Everyone enjoys a nice meal now and then regardless of whether they need it. And what about Jane? Newcomers always have lingering hunger from being on the Mother Land. You've always got an appetite after you return."

"Touché, Bryson. Point taken." Peter couldn't help chuckling at the boy. "But you may have to teach them a thing or two."

"Gee, ya think?" He folded his arms across his chest.

"And be patient."

"Now you're asking too much."

"And politely eat what others cook even if it doesn't look edible."

Bryson eyed Peter, his eyes unflinching.

Peter chuckled again and slapped the boy on the back. "Thank you, Bryson. I knew I could count on you." Peter opened his mouth to say more but stopped himself. "I'm going to get Jane."

"Wait, you're leaving now?"

"Yes." Peter turned and began to walk away.

"Peter, wait. You're not taking her to see the mermaids, are you?"

Peter turned to face him. "She'll have to see everything. Don't worry, though. I'll be careful." Peter could see the concern in the boy's eyes, and it increased his own apprehension, especially given his last encounter with the creatures.

"Thanks again, Bryson."

"Don't mention it." He glared at Peter with a different sort of look now, perhaps skeptical and a bit threatening. "You'd better take care of her."

"I will," Peter responded without thinking about what that really meant or would entail. All he cared about was moving closer to his escape.

Peter followed the sound of Charlie's little voice, hoping that would lead him to Jane as well. It did. A rain cloud had formed—not an uncommon thing in Spring Quarter—and sprinkled lightly over Hollow Tree Wood.

"There's one," Jane said, pointing to a tiny puddle on the ground. She and Charlie ran to it, and each took a turn jumping in. Peter watched in wonder. She'd rested so little since she'd come and never seemed to shed an ounce of energy or enthusiasm. She lifted Charlie and spun him around. Dancing-in-the-rain-Jane. The sight lifted Peter's spirits, but it took a moment for him to realize that his smile felt larger than normal, larger than even its capacity. He shook the smile away, looking around to see if anyone had noticed him watching her like that. But it had been innocent enough. She made him smile. So did all the others at one time or another.

"Jane," Peter called, still trying to keep from smiling at her.

"Oh, we must be in trouble, Charlie. Peter sounds so serious."

"We don't get in trouble. Not from Peter. Only from pirates," Charlie said.

"Pirates?" Jane looked to Peter. She still held a wet Charlie on her left hip. "What pirates? Captain Hook?" She made her right hand look like a hook and playfully swiped at Charlie's face. "Arrrgh, I'll get you, my pretty. Okay, I clearly can't talk like a pirate."

Peter broke into a laugh. He'd never seen a poorer imitation of a pirate. While Peter lost himself in a moment of humor, Jane grew serious.

"Are there really pirates? Are they dangerous?"

"Mostly they're adventurous!" Charlie said. "I once saved Peter from the pirates when they'd beaten him black and blue."

Peter swallowed and began shifting his feet, not knowing quite what to say. Charlie's outbursts could be entirely too revealing, and Peter was surprised Charlie remembered that. At least the nightmares had stopped.

"Has he shown you the branding on his shoulder?" Charlie said.

"Branding?" Jane asked.

Bryson rushed in and reached for Charlie. "Okay, you. Time for a nap."

"No it's not," Charlie protested.

Peter watched Bryson with gratitude. He'd already stepped up and taken Lester's place. Peter watched the duo retreat to Charlie's tree where the young boy would most likely be getting a lecture about talking too much.

"Yes, Jane, there are pirates. Would you like to see? I want to show you the mermaids too. And the fairies again." He studied her face. Her skin had grown smoother since being on Neverland if that was possible. Her dark, tinted hair remained the same as when they'd met, not a fraction of an inch longer, but still angled so one side hung lower than the other. The cut and color of her hair had always stood out to Peter as symbols of her charisma and individuality. Her expression frightened him, though. Was he losing her trust?

"Peter, I feel a warning in my heart."

This statement perplexed him. He tried to think if he'd ever felt that way. He was well-acquainted with fear and apprehension but never would have described those emotions as a warning in his heart. "What do you mean?"

"I don't know." She looked away, as if she kept a secret of her own. Glancing back to him, she spoke again. "Peter, I vaguely remember you telling me Neverland is a safe place."

"It is safe, Jane. Once you know all its secrets. That's what I'd like to show you now." He held out his hand to her and regretted it immediately, fearing the touch of her skin would boggle his mind. He wondered if there was some way to take it back without appearing foolish.

She gazed at his hand but did not take it. This both relieved and puzzled Peter. "I'll go with you," she said. "But I'd like a weapon."

She stared him in the eye, that fearless spark ever present even amid her apprehension.

"Of course, Jane. I already have something in mind." Part of him wanted to ask her if she still thought him capable of harm, but he decided to save that question for another time.

They walked toward his hollow tree, and Peter opened the door for her. She walked in, and it suddenly struck him how selfish he'd been not to assign her a hollow tree yet. Everyone needed rest now and then, not to mention a place of their own. Perhaps he'd simply thought she could take over his tree once he left, but that seemed a poor excuse for not providing her with one already.

Peter walked to a desk near the tree's only window on the first level.

"These trees are amazing," she said, turning in a circle while looking around at every space and crevice.

"Indeed. Have I told you about the hollow trees?"

"No." She turned to him, her interest piqued.

He opened the desk and began to rummage through it. "Hollow trees grow wider than they do tall for much of their lifespan. They eventually begin to hollow out in the center, until there is room for us to live inside. They continue to enlarge, providing more and more space. The sick hollow tree, where you stayed when you first came, is currently the oldest and largest hollow tree."

Finding the knife and the black fairy dust, he closed the drawer and faced her again. "When it is ready to die, a hollow tree will let out a sorrowful groan that goes on and on. That is our signal to vacate the tree, for once it has had enough of pain and sorrow, it will burst into flames and burn itself to the ground."

Her wide eyes showed her amazement, and perhaps a smidgen of disbelief. "Are you for real?"

"Yes, Jane. I am real. This is all real. Would you like a hollow tree of your own? I think I've been foolish not to give you one yet."

"My own hollow tree? Um, of course."

Peter smiled, relieved that she wanted one. "Fantastic. How about we pick one out when we get back?"

"Peter, how long do you think I've been here?"

The question startled him. He breathed deep and determined to answer all questions from here on out truthfully. One hundred percent truthfully. "It's hard to say exactly, Jane. I've yet to master keeping track of Earth time when I'm here, but if I had to guess, I'd say weeks, perhaps a month or more."

"How can it have been that long?"

Peter shrugged in answer. "Here." He held out the knife, hoping to distract her from such a finicky topic as time. "It's the sharpest blade in all of Neverland, or so says the Tally Man at least. And this is black fairy dust, collected from the darkest fairies, those trapped in a deep depression. If you sprinkle it on someone, they will collapse into a stupor of sorrow, so overcome by grief that you will have plenty of time to get far away. I've even seen it be deadly before." He bowed his head at the thought, remembering the pirate whose body he'd come across after first using the black dust as a weapon. The pirate had writhed and wallowed when first being exposed to the dust, moaning and crying so hard he begged for mercy when Peter glanced back. "Be careful not to touch it yourself, though. Here." Peter pulled a wooden box from under his desk and pulled out his last pair of gloves. They were a bit worn since he used them often when chopping or performing other tasks. He handed them to Jane. "Keep these with you. But be careful handling them after exposure to black fairy dust. Otherwise, you could find it hard to function for a while. They can be washed if you have access to water, or you can discard them. We can always ask the Tally Man for more."

She took the gloves, her eyes averting Peter's gaze. "Let me grab my bag." She turned and walked out of Peter's tree, leaving the door open. Peter sucked in a breath and ran his hands through his hair. This was it.

Jane had seemed so tense, even upset, but Peter was afraid to ask her about it. He wondered if she was beginning to think of home, or perhaps Earth had been on her mind for a while now. Maybe the potential dangers caused her anxiety. Peter shook his head and joined Jane outside, where Timothy, Frank and Simon wrestled. He was determined to move forward, distract her, convince her to stay.

"Boys are so dumb," Misty said.

Jane looked toward Peter, and he wondered if she agreed with the statement. What could she possibly think of him? He'd been so secretive, not to mention clumsy with words, and plain dumbstruck in her presence at times. He wondered if he'd ever get the nerve to ask her.

"I heard that, Misty," Bryson said. "And I'm insulted. Drop and give me twenty."

Misty rolled her eyes and walked to her hollow tree.

"Don't let them out of your sight," Peter said to Bryson.

"Where are you going, Peter?" Preston asked.

"We're going away for a bit. Checking on the pirates."

"Ooooh, is this a date?" Timothy asked. "Peter and Jane sitting in a tree. K-I-S-S-I-N-G . . ."

"How in the Neverland stars do you remember that pesky tune?" Bryson asked.

Peter stole a glance at Jane. His cheeks burned, but she seemed unaffected. Her stoicism made him grateful for some reason.

"Don't worry, Timothy. I'll cut his throat if he tries to kiss me."

The warmth drained from Peter's face, and a chill shot through him. Jane sounded completely serious. He began to wonder if *he* was safe.

"You're not taking her to see the mermaids, are you?" Preston asked, his voice edged with concern.

"He said he was," Jane confirmed.

"Peter, that's dangerous," Simon said. All the Lost Boys glared at him, looking either fearful or accusing.

"C'mon, boys. You don't think Jane's afraid of a few vindictive mermaids, do you? We'll be fine."

"But Peter, don't mermaids capture any girl they discover on Neverland?" Frank asked.

Peter rolled his eyes. He had to get away from all these nosy, chattering children before they ruined everything. He'd sincerely hoped to be the one to tell Jane about that.

"Peter, is that true?" Jane asked.

"Yes, Jane. That's why we will stay at a distance. You'll be perfectly safe."

"Is that why there are only Lost Boys?" Jane asked. "What about Misty?"

"Typically, the mermaids will torment any female that comes to Neverland. The only exception is if she is near enough to a boy that he can mask her scent. That's why you've been safe—because you came with me. And that's how Misty survived coming to Neverland."

"Boys are smelly," Misty called from her tree. "It's sometimes a blessing."

They all laughed at this, and Peter knew it would be the perfect time to get away from all the delays.

"You'll be safe as long as you're with me," Peter said. "Let's go."

He walked away from the crowd, and Jane followed, telling Bryson to give Charlie a kiss from her when he woke up. Peter glanced back to see Bryson watching him with that same skepticism. He almost couldn't handle it anymore and reveled in the thought that it would soon be over; he'd tell them all and then be gone.

"Are we walking around the entire planet?" Jane asked. "Can't we fly?"

Peter smiled at these questions. First, he found it charming. Neverland's size was tiny compared to Earth's, and they really could walk the entire thing without too much trouble, especially considering the lighter gravitational pull. Second, he could tell she really just wanted to fly for the fun of it.

"I'm trying to ration fairy dust a bit, but I'm sure we'll fly at some point."

"Oh." She sounded disappointed. "Why are you rationing? Is there a shortage?"

"Perhaps ration isn't the best word. Conserve. We choose to conserve it because it's a precious commodity. Speaking of commodity." He stopped in his tracks when he saw a trail of smoke rising into the sky. "I think I know where we'll visit first."

"What is it?" Jane asked, halting beside Peter.

"A fire. Must be the Tally Man. He's the only one who'd stay in our neck of the woods. He's the only one who'd be brave enough to light a fire where we could see it."

"Who is he?" She adjusted her bag on her shoulder, and Peter wanted to offer to carry it for her but resisted.

He looked Jane severely in the eye, trying to express the importance of the piece of knowledge coming. "He's his own man. He's not on our side, and he's not on the pirates' side or the mermaids' side. He looks after himself alone. We give him what he asks for as long as he's providing supplies and doesn't let the children see him drunk. Beyond that, we don't ask questions. He's not our spy, and he's not theirs. We don't trust him for anything except trade. Do you understand?"

Jane nodded. "I think so. He's useful, but not loyal. Not friendly."

Peter nodded in return. He thought her description was the perfect way to put it. "Ready to meet him?"

Jane didn't respond. Peter watched the side of her face. She swallowed and bit her bottom lip.

"It's okay," he said. "I'm here."

THE TALLY MAN

"Tally-ho, Tally Man," Peter called from a distance, not wanting to frighten the man by sneaking up on him. He'd never make that mistake again.

"Peter, come here. I have much for you." The Tally Man stood and made his way to the tent set up near the fire.

"That's the Tally Man?" Jane asked.

"Not what you expected?"

"I guess I thought he'd be more intimidating, but I have to admit that a spiky-haired Asian man shorter than I am doesn't fit the bill."

Peter laughed out loud.

"What?" Jane asked. "I'm being serious."

"I know you are, it's just . . ."

"What?"

He shrugged. "You're funny."

"I'm funny?"

"Yes."

"Hmm."

"What?" Peter asked. He watched her eyes crinkle as her lips curved into a smile.

"Nothing. Let's go meet this Tally Man." She shook her hands as if mocking the idea that she'd ever found him frightening.

"No, really. What?" He genuinely wanted to know her thoughts, what she kept from him.

"I guess I find it funny that you find me funny. Or anything for that matter. You're usually so serious."

She was right. Peter knew it, even if nobody had ever told him quite so bluntly before. He knew the Lost Boys thought the same thing. Aging had crept up on him, allowing Peter to keep many childlike qualities, but a severity presented itself after Sven had branded him. It became difficult to laugh, hard to focus. The childlike qualities seemed to be slipping away. Since then, he was not someone to turn to for frivolity or sarcasm.

"Well, thanks for the compliment," Peter said. "I think." Jane seemed to be able to bring out the kid in him, which was one of the reasons he loved being around her.

"Anytime." She walked ahead of him, the outline of her figure illuminated by the light of the fire. He couldn't wait to see her in Summer Quarter, where the sun shone bright. Even though one's eyes adjusted to the constant dimness of dawn, Peter knew the light of the full Neverland sun would reveal anything about Jane he'd been missing—any unique glances or mannerisms, any flaws. How he hoped to find some flaws—they might just shake any fondness for her from his mind. On second thought, he'd always be fond of her. She came with him to Neverland. If all went according to plan, she would be the one to save him from this place. Peter followed behind, his thoughts turning to the pirates.

"Tally Man, are the pirates on Neverland?"

"I thought you said you didn't ask about the pirates?" Jane asked through her teeth.

"No, they are still on planet Earth. Or on the Mother Ship as you like to say."

Peter gave Jane a wide grin. He'd told her the bleakest things about the Tally Man, not the humorous ones.

The man twitched his finger in Peter's direction. "Ah, Peter is being naughty. Trying to get secret from the Tally Man."

Peter leaned toward Jane. "He always answers our questions at first, before he even knows what he's doing."

Jane looked at Peter with a half-smile and raised eyebrows.

"Go on. Ask him something," Peter said.

"Tally Man, when will the pirates be coming back?" Jane asked.

"They told me soon." The Tally Man covered his mouth after realizing his blunder. "They told me not to tell you that. Peter's friend is naughty too."

Peter laughed. "As you can see, we generally have nothing to fear from the Tally Man. As long as we remember that he probably gives away some of our secrets too. 'Mum's the word' around him."

"What you say, Peter? You want mum? I didn't bring any flower. What you want mum for?"

"No, we don't want any mums. But we will take any food you can spare, or animals. And Frank could use a new suit."

"Do you know how much a suit cost? Even one his size? You will owe me, Peter."

"I know, Tally Man. Put it on my tab."

The man went back inside his tent, mumbling and shaking his head.

Peter glanced at Jane, who took all of this in with grace. How did she do it? He wondered how much her ability to cope was due to her own personality and how much was the effect of being on Neverland. He chose to think it had everything to do with her.

Coming back out, the man held a rooster in one arm and a goat in the other. "Here. You can have these." He placed them down and went back inside.

"How often will he answer the questions you ask?"

"Every time."

"Seriously?"

"We've been guilty of making a game of it more than once before. He does get mad on occasion though, if he suspects we're doing it on purpose. He stayed away for several moon phases once. And you don't ever want to see his hot temper."

"Peter, tell me about the moon cycles," Jane said. "I thought you said time didn't exist here. Isn't a moon cycle a way of counting time?"

"Not here. The moon phases are irregular and have to do with the fairy queen. They change according to her mood, so it's not predictable. You can feel it though, if you learn how to tune in to the atmosphere."

The Tally Man's return did not pull Jane from her thoughts. Peter understood. It had taken ages for him to learn all of this. He still remembered how strange some of Neverland's features seemed at first.

"Here you go. One box of food."

"How much for you to deliver all of it to the Lost Boys? They'd love it if you stopped by."

"Peter, no need to flatter me. I can deliver. No charge."

"You're so good to us, Tally Man. What would we do without you?"

Jane spoke through her teeth. "They're literally a hundred feet away."

Peter leaned close to her and whispered. "He thrives on praise and compliments. It's business. Try it. He'll love you forever." Peter hesitated to pull away. He found being that close to Jane both thrilled him and comforted him.

She pulled back to question him. "Really?"

Peter nodded.

"Tally Man, you are a wonder among men," Jane said.

"Oh, stop," he said, waving a hand at her and laughing.

"I'm sure we'd perish without your brave deeds," she added.

Peter laughed at her. "Okay, don't overdo it."

"What? I thought those were good."

"Peter, who is she? She look familiar to me." He put the box down and came closer to them. "I'm sure I've seen her face before."

Peter looked to Jane, who turned away in a momentary fluster. He could see her discomfort, but she rebounded almost instantly.

"Guess I've just got one of those faces." She shrugged. "What about you, Tally Man? Where are you from?"

He looked to Peter, as if to ask what she meant.

"I'm from Earth." He looked at them as though this should be obvious. "Nobody is born on Neverland."

Jane opened her mouth to respond, but stopped, as if his comment had sent her deep into another necessary contemplation.

"I think she means where on Earth are you from. What country or region perhaps?" Peter looked to Jane for confirmation, but her preoccupation kept her from hearing him.

"Oh, that. I knew that. I'm from Thailand." He placed his fists on his hips and faced them with pride.

Jane snapped out of her stupor. "Thailand! Oh, how exotic."

"Not really," the Tally Man said. "Not compared to Neverland anyway."

"Well I was born in New Jersey," Jane said.

The Tally Man grinned widely, then changed the subject. "Peter, your tab is getting high." Though he continued to smile, Peter could sense his emotions shifting. He imagined him as a bright-yellow fairy, the color of irritation.

"Yes, I know. Perhaps I can make ready some dust for your next trip?"

"I think that would be wise."

"What are you most in need of?"

"I'm out of helplessness. And I'd like a puff of anxiety, depression, for enemies. And you owe me a heap of joy."

"Sounds like you're running a fairy pharmacy," Jane said.

"No drugs. Tally Man don't do drugs. No need with fairy dust. Keeps my enemies away, keeps me happy, and keeps me coming to Neverland whenever I want so I can stay young."

"The good life indeed," Peter said. He pulled out a notebook and pen to write down the Tally Man's request. "Well, we'd better be on our way. I'm showing Jane around the place."

The Tally Man's face contorted into a look of concern. "Peter, you are not taking her to see mermaids, are you?"

"I'm starting to get a little worried about these mermaids."

Peter looked at Jane, who appeared to have said it with more sarcasm than anything.

"I'll make sure she stays safe. It's better she knows the dangers."

"Peter is so wise. Except when he's not." The man shuffled about, organizing a few items before sitting down in front of the fire.

"See you later, Tally Man."

Jane leaned over and whispered, "Doesn't he have a real name?"

"No idea," Peter whispered back. "That's what he asked us to call him."

"Oh, you two whisper close like a pair of turtle doves."

Peter looked at Jane. She seemed to be forcing back a laugh, but Peter's cheeks grew hot.

"Do turtle doves whisper?" she asked. "Who knew?"

"Let's go," Peter said. Getting away from the Tally Man seemed of utmost importance all of a sudden. He led Jane through his camp and into the woods once more. They walked in silence at first, but Peter knew the questions would come soon. And he had some of his own now. Hearing of her birthplace piqued his interest. He wanted to know more about her. Everything even. How else could he justify leaving the Lost Boys with her?

"Peter?"

Here came the questions.

"Is what he said true? Babies aren't born on Neverland?"

"Human babies aren't." They climbed a wooded hill as Peter explained. "Think about how a human being can live here forever and never age a day. The plants and animals that are native here can breed and die, and from what I've seen, their life cycles and reproduction timelines are much different from Earth's breeds and vegetation. Plants and animals that come from Earth can die, but they don't age. I'm not sure what causes it, but it's like life cells native to Earth remain unchanged here. Ever notice how many eggs we eat? Even though we have plenty of hens and roosters?"

"I never thought about it."

"The roosters will still attempt to fertilize the eggs, and the hens will sometimes collect the eggs and even attempt to hatch them. The instincts remain, but nothing happens to begin cell division. There are never any chicks."

Jane chuckled. "Better keep this place a secret. Otherwise, people will come in flocks just for the birth control. Forget about living forever."

His cheeks flushed again. The startling effects of her words began to annoy him. Why couldn't she just shut up and stop being so alluring?

"Tell me more about the moon cycle. And how is it I've gone a month without sleeping?"

"I've already told you all I know about the moon. It's always a full moon and its color changes depending on the moods of the queen. Sometimes it will stay the same general color but vary in shades. It will get darker or lighter depending on how long the queen stays in her mood."

"So if she is angry, the moon is red or something?"

"Yes, and if she gets less angry, it will lighten in color a bit. It may even switch to orange if the anger dissipates enough. And there are no months here. Actually, I'm surprised you haven't needed sleep yet. Usually, when someone comes for the first time, sleep is more frequent than it is for those of us who have been here for a while."

"What about Charlie? He sleeps all the time."

"True. He's young, though. And he really hasn't been here much longer than you."

Jane stopped. They'd been walking side-by-side, Jane's hands grasping the straps of her backpack, but now she stared at him, eyes wide and unflinching. "You mean he just recently lost his parents?" He could see the empathy in her concerned brow, and how much she cared for him. "And we've left him? He needs us to stay close by."

Peter stepped toward her, wanting to console. "Neverland has other effects, and so does the fairy dust. There is a forgetfulness here. It isn't as difficult as you might think. For example, do you miss your parents?"

"My parents?" She looked off into the distance. "I think I remember. When the Tally Man told me that I looked familiar to him, I remembered. It made me uneasy that he recognized me, but I couldn't quite understand why until now. My parents are famous, and pictures of my face have graced the front pages of tabloids from time to time. I didn't want him to make the connection. That's why I changed the subject."

Peter began to process all of this. He wanted to press for more information but somehow sensed it would be better to wait.

"And no, I don't miss them." She began walking again and brushed past him, her curiosity replaced by annoyance, or so it would seem.

They walked in silence for a time until something seemed to dawn on Jane.

"Peter, if there is no true moon cycle, no changing of day to night, does that mean there are never any sunrises?"

"On the contrary. Look ahead." He pointed to the top of a hill where the forest ended.

Eager to see what he referred to, she climbed the hill in earnest, taking quick, careful steps as she avoided rocks and divots. Her hands clasped around the straps of her backpack again, and her hair waved back and forth. She gasped when she reached the top.

"I see it! I can see the sunshine!"

Peter stood beside her. "Breathtaking, isn't it?"

A vast, grassy meadow stretched out before them, spotted with every color of flower imaginable. Some resembled poppies, others daisies, and others were completely unique to Neverland. Partway through the meadow rested the line between Spring and Summer Quarters, the line between dawn and daybreak that never moved.

Letting out a hearty laugh, Jane jogged down into the meadow. She kept running all the way until crossing the line and threw herself down into the bed of long grass and flowers. He knew how she felt. Nothing compared to sunshine. If the pirates hadn't claimed this quarter first, Peter would have built a home for the Lost Boys here. Still, as great as the warmth would feel on his skin, he always took the sunrise with gradualness. He slowed rather than speeding up, allowing the light to creep in rather than overtake him. He stretched out his arms and watched the light increase gradually, his sight adjusting through squinted eyes.

Jane had taken off her backpack and rested face up, arms open wide. "And it will never go down?"

"Not as long as we stay here."

"Awesome. Let's stay forever." She closed her eyes. Peter looked down at her, taking in all of her curves and edges in the full light of sun. He'd never noticed the slight dimple in her left cheek or the small birthmark on her neck.

He cleared his throat, trying to shove his mind away from the thoughts slipping inexplicably into his head. Thoughts of kisses and Jane's arms around him. He shook his head, desperately grasping for a distraction, something else to think about.

"Let's keep moving." Peter began walking again.

Jane sat up. "But we just got here. Can't we enjoy it?"

"We can enjoy it while we walk."

"Oh, you're no fun."

"I know." He couldn't keep the smile from his lips. He looked back to see her swing her backpack onto her shoulders. "I could carry that for you." He didn't know what had possessed him to say something so stupid. It's not like it would be heavy.

"Thanks, but I can barely feel it. This low gravity thing is pretty amazing. Is that part of why we're traveling so fast? Or is Neverland super tiny?"

"Gravity has a lot to do with it. It's not as small as it seems. We're able to travel much faster and cover more ground because of the gravity factor. It also helps that there is no calculating of time, so it doesn't feel like it has taken long to walk through an entire quarter." Her questions served as the perfect distraction, and Peter was glad.

"And the pirates live here?"

"On the other end, yes. There are some cliffs overlooking an ocean. Their ship is usually anchored near there."

"What's the ocean like?"

He exhaled a small laugh. "It's an ocean."

"Do you think the pirates will be back by now?"

Peter shrugged. "Who knows? Could be."

"Do you think the Lost Boys miss me? And Misty? Poor thing, I've left her with all those rowdy boys."

Peter laughed again. "She'll be fine. She's used to it. Having another girl around is a novelty for her."

She rested her mouth for a few beats. "Peter, why is it that the mermaids are dangerous for girls?"

This question caused a knot to form in Peter's gut. He wanted to avoid telling her all their dangers as long as possible. "It's just jealousy, really. They can't stand the thought of having other women here."

"But what would they do to me?"

Peter stopped and turned to her. "Don't worry about that now. I promise I'll keep you safe. They know me well. They won't hurt you if I ask them not to." Peter only knew it to be a lie after he'd said it. Unwilling to take it back, he allowed the falsehood to calm her. Somehow the possibility of Jane being in danger began to cause him anxiety, but Peter couldn't say why.

"Well, that's comforting I guess." Her eyes searched his, her intense look causing him increasing discomfort. "You're not very forthcoming, are you?"

He broke eye contact. "No, I suppose not. What is the word? Introverted, I guess."

"I noticed." She grinned, placing her hands in the pockets of her jeans, which still sported mud stains from their sliding adventure. Had he been anyone else, Peter might have wished he'd brought some calming fairy dust or something else to quiet his companion a bit. With Jane, however, he was learning that he didn't mind so much. She could talk forever, and he would be content to listen, answer her questions, and just have her close.

A Pirate Farm

"*P*eter, it's stifling. I think I need something to drink."

He looked around to see how far they'd gone. "There's a stream near here. Let's head this way for a bit." He led them off to the right in the direction of the stream and reached into his pocket, the silky feel of the fairy dust lifting his mood and quickly helping his own temperature adjust to the heat. "Here. This will help." He paused to sprinkle a little on top of her head and found it difficult to pull his hand away from her. He'd been trying to keep his distance, but sometimes closeness couldn't be avoided. He thanked the Never stars he'd brought plain old gold fairy dust rather than something as impractical as magenta, the color for passion. He jerked away from her and began moving his feet once more.

The stream ran through an open meadow, surrounded on both sides with thick blades of perfect green grass that only grew to just above his ankles. Jane knelt and cupped the clear water into her hands. She slurped the water up, drops falling down her hands, arms, and chin. She dipped a hand back in the water and flicked some of it on her face and then turned to flick some at Peter.

"Feels good," he said, closing his eyes and wiping away the wetness.

Jane threw her hand back into the water and splashed as much as she could in Peter's direction. "How does that feel?"

He closed his eyes again but did not bother to wipe the water away. Debating whether to let it drop or throw her in the stream, he felt another wave of water hit his face, drenching his hair.

"That's it." He opened his eyes and wasted no time grasping her around the waist and lowering her into the stream, backpack and all. She'd looked surprised when he grabbed her, but sitting in the water, knees bent, and hair pasted to her face, she looked pleased.

"Peter, I never thought you'd stoop so low."

"Well, sometimes I can't help it when provoked." He could feel the smile on his face, enormous and sincere, and he also couldn't help noticing the way her hair glistened in the Never sunlight. Clearing his throat, he turned away. "We should get going."

"Why? Why are you always in such a hurry?"

"Am I?" He turned to see her with her arms wrapped around her knees. The stream carried on, not caring in the slightest about the detour it had to take around her thighs and feet.

"Yes, you are. And I demand to know why." She stuck her chin out in mock defiance.

"Let me guess. You're not moving from that spot until I tell you?" Peter asked.

She nodded once.

"Fine. Get wet. Doesn't matter now that I've showered you with fairy dust. You can probably barely feel it."

"Oh, all right. Let's keep moving then." She began to stand, and Peter reached his hand out to help her, again flustered as to why he would do so; lifting off the ground was nothing, especially now that she had some fairy dust on her person. Perhaps they'd fly for a bit, pick up the pace even more. Of course, he couldn't say that now; she had already accused him of being in a hurry.

"You're so pushy." For Jane, this probably signified the closest thing to insult she'd ever give, though it couldn't count as an insult when she spoke with such harmless ridicule. "And stubborn."

"I know," Peter said. "I've had over a century to get in touch with each and every one of my flaws."

Jane lifted one foot out of the water followed by the other. She smiled at him, and then her lips straightened, and she put her fingers to her forehead.

"What is it?" Peter asked.

"Nothing, it's just that I feel . . ."

"What? You don't feel sick, do you?" Peter remembered well the moist feeling of her vomit through his shoes.

She looked him in the eye, as if puzzled about whatever realization she was coming to. "I feel tired."

"Oh, well that's better than feeling sick. I'm not surprised. There can be a bit of crashing when fairy dust begins to wear off. Not to mention you haven't slept since you first arrived."

"But where am I going to sleep?"

"I guess that depends. Do you want sun or shade?"

She sat down and covered the yawn escaping her mouth. "I don't know."

"From the looks of it, it's too late to make any plans. Here, let me take your backpack."

"Hmm?" Jane fell onto her side, out cold.

She'd probably never know the difference, but Peter worked to get the backpack off her, hoping it would help her be more comfortable. Not that physical comfort was hard to come by on Neverland. Unless pirates tortured you, it was pretty much a given. After releasing one arm from bondage, he carefully rolled her onto her opposite side to get the other arm out. She pulled away from him and curled her knees to her chest, resting her hands under her cheek. Peter found his hand still resting on her arm, and for once, the urge to rush left him. He wanted to stay there with his hand on her arm, the warmth of her skin beneath his fingertips. Knowing she'd never know, he planted a kiss on her temple. No matter what had caused him to do it, he had to pull away from her, look for a distraction. Given his plans, he could not afford these thoughts, nor the feelings threatening to weaken his determination. The idea of Jane seemed nice, grand even. But more than anything, he needed out.

A distant mooing caught his attention, and he looked to the other side of the stream, where a handful of cows approached. He let go of Jane and stood, turning to take in the landscape all around. Visiting Summer Quarter always proved refreshing. He couldn't deny that he'd missed this: time to himself. With Jane sleeping and nothing but a few cows surrounding, he welcomed the solitude.

Peter liked having animals on Neverland but shuddered when he thought of how Sven used the Mermaid passage to get them. It required too much blood in Peter's opinion, but the mermaids didn't concern themselves with such things. Passage fares through the portal they used to get from Earth to Neverland were beyond Peter's reach—morally and emotionally. But what did Sven care about killing a few innocents?

As the cows approached, Peter began to hear the soft clanging of their bells, followed by the bleating of a few lambs following the crowd. He pulled out his journal and took a few notes, careful not to include anything about Jane. At least, nothing much. Just how she'd interpreted the Tally Man, how she'd asked endless questions, how she'd splashed him twice, and how she'd fallen asleep on the grass practically mid-sentence. Nothing about his feelings though. Nothing about how pleasant she could be. And facetious. Just like her eyes. None of that. Part of him wanted to remember, and another faction was already trying to forget.

He stopped writing and sketched her lying there by the stream, the cows drinking on the other side, until she finally woke.

She didn't rub her eyes or wake one gradual moment at a time. She bolted up and turned her head to the cows. "How long have I been asleep?"

"You ask that like I have a watch on my wrist."

She smiled "Right. How long do you think I slept?"

"I'm not answering that."

"Why not?"

"It's good for you. The sooner you realize that time has no purpose or even existence here, the better. Then perhaps you'll stop pestering me about it." Yet *he* couldn't keep his mind off it. Every passing moment seemed to take him further from his destination, especially the moments he spent with her.

"Well done, Peter. I think you just sampled some sarcasm. How did it taste coming off your tongue?"

"Pretty bland, actually."

"You're pathetic. What's with the cows, by the way?"

"They belong to the pirates."

"Seriously?" She found this humorous apparently.

Peter shrugged. "A pirate's got to eat."

"Speaking of food. I could use a bite I think."

"Got a gun? We could shoot a cow and light a fire."

"Peter, I'm shocked. You do have a sense of humor."

He laughed at her accusation. "No, I don't. I was being serious."

Jane looked at the cows. "I'm not that hungry anymore." She leaned back on her hands.

"How did you sleep?" Peter asked.

"Like a baby."

"Did you know that phrase comes from Neverland?"

"What do you mean?"

Peter pulled a blade of grass and played with it as he spoke. A replacement grew in the exact spot, a wonder that Jane didn't even notice. "Babies don't sleep. They wake hungry and crying. They're fitful, and they jerk. They're alert the moment you try to leave the room. But on Neverland, a baby sleeps as if they will never wake again."

She sat up straight and crossed her legs. "Seriously? Are there other phrases that come from Neverland?"

"There are dozens. This one really isn't a phrase, just a line in a nursery rhyme, but ever heard of the cow that jumped over the moon?" Peter nodded his head toward the animals across the stream.

"Yeah."

"Just give a cow a little fairy dust and a shove over to Winter Quarter, and there you have it."

Jane burst into laughter. She threw herself back and rolled in the grass, holding her stomach as she went on and on.

Peter had no idea he could be so humorous. And the idea of a cow flying through the air didn't faze him. He'd seen it often enough; making the animals fly served as one of the best entertainments in Neverland, especially back when the pirates could take a joke.

His discomfort grew because the laughter continued to ring out as though it would never stop. He stood up and hopped across the stream. "You coming? We've got a pirate farm to see. And an ocean."

She kept laughing, so Peter did the only thing he could think of— walked on without her, passing through the animals dotting the field. A group of hens pecked at his feet. Animals seemed fine without food on Neverland, and perhaps that included chickens, though the lack of something to eat didn't keep them from pecking at the ground.

"I don't have anything, ladies. Sorry." He stopped and glanced back at Jane who was finally getting up and retrieving her backpack. The laughter continued, lighter than before and drifting, but still echoing across the Neverland air and ringing like a joyful bell in Peter's ears.

"I'm coming," she hollered. She reached him breathless, her smile brighter than the Never sun. "That . . . is the funniest thing I've ever heard."

"So I see." He began walking again.

She jumped into step with him. "Get it? Herd. As in a herd of cows?"

He chuckled out of courtesy. "That was worse than Timothy's chicken joke."

"Yeah, it was, wasn't it?"

The cliffs came into view, and at seeing their black, jagged edges, fear sent its tentacles through Peter's chest, grappling for a place to take hold. He slowed, maybe even stalled. Panic threatened to seize him, and his heart began to race.

"What's wrong?" Jane asked.

"Nothing, why?" He took his breaths faster, braving a look at her.

"You're not the only one who can sense mood changes."

He took a deep breath and smoothed his hair back, contemplating the idea of sitting down for a rest. No, he had to keep moving. Pausing to dwell on memories even for a moment could make things worse. And he had to hide his emotions better; Jane could never see him panic. "I'm fine." He imagined seeing the ocean, the crashing waves, the endless sparkles like glitter floating on the water. Forcing his feet forward, he focused on every step, his eyes watching his shoes smother the perfect grass. He pictured seeing the water, one of the only things left near the pirates that he could enjoy. That and the flying animals.

"Peter?"

Best to change the subject. Act as though he'd never almost lost it in front of her. "Do you want to hear some other phrases that come from Neverland? Ever heard 'When pigs fly?'"

Jane halted. Peter turned to see her, and the look on her face startled him. "I'm not taking another step until you tell me."

"Tell you what?" Peter stared toward her, trying above all to avoid her eyes.

Hands on her hips, she glared in his direction, biting her lip and huffing as she looked to her surroundings. "Whatever. Keep your secrets."

Grateful she hadn't pushed it, but also regretting that he'd annoyed her at the very least, he watched her move past him and toward the cliffs.

"Why were you running away?" Peter called after her. He couldn't quite say what had brought on the question. He'd resolved to wait, but the words leapt from his mouth. Perhaps he truly wanted to share with her how this place scared him above all others, and he would find that easier if she shared something first.

She turned to face him. "Will you tell me why you tensed up?"

Peter nodded.

She searched the sky for a moment. Was she trying to remember? He wondered how much she had forgotten already. Of course, it seemed the younger the child, the more forgetful. Perhaps Jane's memories of her Earth life and home remained clear. After a sharp inhale, she began. "My parents are getting divorced. Not that I care, really. I found out by reading the paper. Some of my friends knew before I did." She bowed her head. "But none of that really matters. Nor is any of it surprising."

"So, what happened?" Peter waited.

"About three months ago . . . No, that's all wrong now."

"It's okay," Peter said. "Forget about Neverland and just tell it the way you normally would."

Jane took another sharp inhale and nodded her head. "About three months before coming here, I came home to an eviction notice. Not only that, but my nanny had left a note saying she'd been let go, and she left immediately to find work elsewhere. I don't think my parents had paid her for months."

"But she left without saying good-bye?"

Jane's face reddened, and a tear fell down her cheek. She shrugged. "Maybe she couldn't bear to. That's what I tell myself. She's the only family I've ever really known."

Peter couldn't bear to see her cry. He thought about offering her some more fairy dust. "I'm sorry," he said. "I'm sure she found the thought of leaving too painful if shared with you."

Jane folded her arms. Peter marveled at this girl. She'd been running away—not by choice but out of necessity. As more tears came, Jane wiped them, then released one strap of her backpack and began rummaging through it. She pulled out a package of gum, selected a piece, unwrapped it, and folded it into her mouth. "Want some? It always helps me feel better."

He smiled at her. "Sure, why not?" He took a piece and set it on his tongue, beginning to chew as the bursts of peppermint flavor reached his taste buds. "Thank you," he said. "I haven't tasted anything like that in a long time." He watched her pull a jacket from her backpack and slide it on. It must have been for comfort since jackets weren't needed in Summer Quarter. Peter's admiration for her continued to grow. It eased his mind that she needed Neverland possibly as much as it needed her. But what about Peter? Could he do without Jane? Of course he could. "The flavor suits you," he said, trying to escape this conversation and his current thoughts. "Sweet-as-a-candy-cane-Jane." He hoped she'd forgotten that he'd promised some information in exchange.

"Now, Peter. What is it that has you so unnerved?" She sniffed and wiped away the last of the tears, seemingly anxious to embrace the forgetfulness that awaited her here.

Peter took a moment to stand still and notice the breeze passing across his forehead and arms. He took a deep breath. "Before you came to Neverland, the pirates brought me here for torture. I haven't been quite the same since. This place scares me more than anything else."

"Is that when they branded you?"

"Yes."

"Could I see it?"

Peter took a deep breath and reached for his shirt sleeve. He lifted it to reveal the mark left by Sven before Peter ever knew of Jane's existence. He hesitated to look at her, afraid of her reaction.

Jane studied the brand, then grasped his arm and rubbed her thumb across the scarring, her touch commanding Peter's attention. She looked at him with compassion, or was it pity? Peter couldn't bear the thought of her pitying him.

"Well, then," she said. "Let's not stay long. That wasn't so hard, was it?"

Yes. Giving her even that minute detail had been excruciating. Her opinion of him grew in importance with every step, or so it seemed. He hoped she didn't think less of him. He couldn't think of anything more humiliating or unpleasant than Jane thinking him a coward, except perhaps Jane being in danger. "Let's keep moving. They could get back anytime."

"Peter, what's that?"

He looked toward the cliff and saw smoke rising from beyond its edge. Jane looked at him. "What do we do?"

Peter observed the alarm in her eyes. "Let's not get caught."

"Should we get back to the Lost Boys? Would the pirates go after them?"

"Maybe, but we're nearly as far away from them as possible. We may as well continue in the same direction. I'll show you where the mermaids live."

"Peter, why haven't we seen any fairies?"

He looked around. Now that he gave it some thought, he realized how strange it was. "I don't know. The queen nests in Summer Quarter, and most of the fairies live here. Let's get going. Maybe we'll see some once we get away from the pirate camp."

"Any chance we could catch a glimpse of their ship? Or the ocean?"

Peter felt an urge to back away from it all: the cliffs, the ocean, the pirates, Jane—who apparently had no fear of this place despite what he'd told her. He shook his head, trying not to give away his reasons. They probably could avoid being seen, but he simply couldn't take a step toward the danger he knew was possible there.

"Okay," she said. "Which way?"

"Let's go past the barn and walk along the cliff edge at a distance until the sun sets."

"It seems way too early for a sunset, but whatever."

She turned and walked toward the ramshackle barn, holding the straps of her backpack. "What's in Autumn Quarter?"

A chill ran up Peter's spine at the thought. They were leaving one danger behind only to embrace another. Perhaps it would be better to turn around completely and go back through Summer and Spring Quarters to get to Hollow Tree Wood.

"Peter?"

"Mermaids."

FRANTIC FAIRIES

*J*ane tromped through a thickening wood. The trees in the near distance had leaves of autumn colors, rather than green, that fell to the ground. Peter looked over his shoulder to see the sun beginning to dip behind the horizon. He could feel it already, a mood shift from Summer to Autumn. Whether it took place because of the fairy queen or the foreboding in his own heart, he couldn't tell.

"Peter, look." Jane stood still, her eyes planted on something to his right. He looked to see a trail of fairy glow on the move. Hundreds, maybe even a thousand or so fairies appeared to be fleeing from Summer Quarter. Peter searched for a memory of having ever seen this before to understand what it meant.

"Maybe they're being hunted. Or caught. Sven's tried it before, but I've never seen so many fleeing at once," Peter said.

"But why is he hunting them?" Jane asked.

Peter watched their colors. Many remained the dark green of worry, but some began to change to something else. A red here, an orange, a brown, a yellow, a gray. But nothing blue or purple. Something had gone wrong.

"They're probably avoiding a pirate trap. Not to worry, though. Fairies are resourceful. They'll be all right."

"Why do the pirates want to trap them?"

"For their dust. When the pirates don't feel like trading the Tally Man for fairy dust, they try to capture them, but pirates aren't patient enough, so Sven invents ways to try to hurry the process."

"They look frantic," Jane said.

"Yes, some of them are. None of them are calm right now. Or happy or peaceful. Stress and worry, anger, fear, confusion."

"Can't we do anything to help them?"

Peter thought about it. Perhaps they could. He reasoned that his fear of the pirates was unfounded. He knew he hadn't been in London for more than a month. Sven wouldn't be hunting him down. Not yet. "C'mon. Let's keep moving," he said. "We'll travel with them. There's a hill in that direction. Let's go see if we can get some of them settled down."

Peter led Jane to a clearing in the wood. On the other side of the clearing they walked up a hill. "Hungry?" Peter asked. They'd left the sun behind, and dusk ruled their current location.

"Actually, I am a little. Or maybe I'm just nervous."

"Because of the fairies?" He handed her a granola bar. She opened it and began to eat.

She nodded, speaking between bites. "And the pirates. And the mermaids." She stared at him for a moment, as if debating whether to keep going. "And you."

Peter raised his eyebrows at this revelation. "Me?"

She nodded. "I can't figure you out, Peter Pan." She sat down at the top of the hill, and Peter realized that perhaps this wasn't the best place for them to sit. Deep in the continuing woods, Peter caught a glimpse of Brim Lake, where the mermaids lived. He doubted the creatures could see him and Jane from the water, let alone be able to tell that a girl sat so close to their lair. His scent would mask hers. Yet, seeing the lake still unnerved him; so much remained for him to learn about mermaids, who had always been the most cryptic creatures on Neverland. While their physical bodies were contained to the water, they seemed to have telepathic powers, and even be able to see the future.

"Aren't you going to sit down?" She gasped and spoke with greater enthusiasm. "Look, Peter. They're slowing down. They're surrounding us."

Pulled from the worry of mermaids for a moment, Peter looked down at her, fairies circling around in glowing hues of nearly every color.

Jane giggled. She held out her hand hoping to touch one. Peter sat down by her. "Here, let me show you." He took her arm and placed the back of her hand in his palm. "Let them see that you welcome them. Let them hear that they're welcome."

"What do you mean?"

"Say something to them. Something to greet or welcome them."

Peter smiled at her. She clearly thought this part strange.

"Like, 'Here, little fairy'?" she asked in a mocking tone.

Peter laughed at her. "It doesn't matter what you say, as long as it's sincere."

"Oh. Well, okay. Here it goes." She leaned forward, focusing on a nearby swarm. "Hello there. Would you like to come and sit with us?" She waited, an eager expression plastered to her face.

Mesmerized, Peter hardly noticed the fairies. Jane seemed to shine brighter than anything he'd ever seen.

"It's not working," Jane said.

"I haven't finished explaining yet." Truthfully, he enjoyed having her hand in his so much, he wanted to keep it that way, slow things down, let hours and weeks and months go by on Earth and keep her here like this. With him. "Now," he began. "Let them feel that they're welcome."

"How am I supposed to do that?"

"Fairies can sense emotion. So if you're feeling angst, your chances are slim, unless of course a fairy feeling angst flies by. In that case, it might come and sit on your hand. Misery loves company."

"Let me guess. That quote comes from Neverland too?"

"Actually, yes."

She smiled wide and closed her eyes.

"That's it," Peter coached. "Focus on what you're feeling. They will be attracted when they feel you are safe, comfortable, peaceful, happy, loving."

With Jane's eyes sealed shut, Peter could stare without the fear of seeming creepy or interested. Her cheeks lacked the summer glow they radiated earlier. He wished to touch her face just the same.

"Okay, I think I'm ready."

Peter realized that his own emotions might be keeping them away. He closed his eyes and tried not to think of Jane, who now had him feeling confused or perhaps filled with longing. Not exactly attractive sentiments to fairies. He thought of Endal Ocean, its glimmering waters and white sands. The perfect blue water. He remembered the time he and the Lost Boys had built a raft and set sail, not expecting a rare storm that left them stranded on an island until Charlie learned to swim. He smiled, and Jane inhaled, sounding surprised. He opened his eyes to see a golden-yellow fairy in her palm. She watched it with glee and awe.

"Look, Peter."

"I see it. Keep watching. It only gets better from here."

"It's changing colors!"

Peter could tell she struggled to contain her excitement. She bounced on the seat of her pants and waved her free hand.

Once yellow, the fairy switched to blue, then maroon, probably matching Jane's excitement, then settled to gold, finally happy at last.

"What does it all mean?" Jane asked. "What was it feeling?"

"Probably everything you were feeling, but it liked the happy emotion best. It seems settled. Hold still." Peter took his free hand and reached into his pack for the velvet sack of gold fairy dust. He opened it one-handed—still not willing to let go of Jane's hand—and loosened the string holding it shut. He held the sack near the fairy, knowing it could take off at any moment. Another fairy landed on Jane's leg, distracting her. Peter let go of Jane's hand and picked up the gold fairy. Squeezing gently, he held the fairy's tail end over the sack and pumped a few times.

"Is that what I think it is?" Jane asked.

"What?"

"Did you just collect that fairy's poop?"

Peter chuckled. "Not exactly. Fairies, and other creatures native to Neverland, don't have the same bodily systems that we do. Fairies produce dust endlessly. That's what we call it anyway, probably because it wouldn't be as desirable if we thought of it as poop. The dust will occasionally just fall out, leaving a trail behind a fairy in flight, but if you want to collect some, all you need is a gentle hand and something to collect it in."

Peter would have given loads of fairy dust away to bottle up the look of wonder on Jane's face.

"That . . . is awesome."

"Pretty extraordinary, aren't they?"

He considered slipping his hand back under hers now, but it seemed unnecessary.

"Oh, hold on," Peter said, securing the string on the velvet sack and putting it back. He reached into his pack for a glove and put it on. "I see a black fairy. Think I'll collect some of that dust while I've got the chance."

He rummaged through his pack looking for the velvet sack with the skull and crossbones on the front. Jane watched him work, still enthralled. He couldn't keep the smile from his face and savored the opportunity to show off his fairy-dust-collecting skills.

Peter finished and discarded the glove. The fairy did not change from black. Often that was the case, though. Once in such a deep despair, fairies often remained in that state until death. Tragic, really.

A nagging question begged to leap from Peter's mouth. He tried to resist, but it wouldn't back down. He wondered why she couldn't figure him out. Peter suspected he already knew the answer. He'd brought her here on his own pretenses, with his own ideas of how to get out of this place. Now everything seemed to be changing. His plans hid behind a fogged glass in his mind. He couldn't figure *himself* out. Or Jane. Or his feelings for her. "Jane, why do I make you nervous?"

Expecting to hear about how she didn't trust him, Peter braced himself. He even tried to resolve to tell the truth if she questioned him.

She shrugged and leaned back on her hands. "Well, I can tell you're attracted to me. I'm on tenterhooks wondering if you're going to break down and kiss me or not."

Peter's face and chest burst into heat.

"It'd be nice to have some warning, by the way," she added. "Then I can say no or run for it if I want to. Don't just plant one on me. That's so gross."

"Umm . . . I—" He couldn't tear his eyes away from her lips now, and he wished he'd never brought it up. "What if I did kiss you?"

She shrugged. "You tell me."

Peter's mind became a jumble of thimbles and kisses. He thought of Wendy, and how he'd hoped she would stay forever. But she didn't. Now he wanted Jane to stay, but he planned to leave. But a kiss was only a kiss.

"I might kiss you," he said.

"I might run away." She raised her eyebrows as if in challenge. He had no idea how she would react to him if he leaned in and puckered up. In fact, she'd hinted that it wouldn't go well at all. Her lips beckoned, and he thought he saw her glance at his mouth in anticipation.

"I'm going to kiss you."

Leaning in, he thought it a good sign that she hadn't answered that one. She remained still, even expressionless until their lips touched. Peter closed his eyes and hoped. She responded, accepting his kiss. Her lips still tasted of peppermint. Though the kissing was pleasurable, Peter knew he couldn't linger. Lingering only brought misery: more longing, harder good-byes, greater attachment, and keener pain.

With intense regret, he pulled away.

"That was a kiss of loneliness," Jane said.

As if to prove her point, a pale-green fairy landed on Peter's knee.

"But how can you be lonely when you're not alone, Peter?" she asked.

He looked into those eyes. They didn't seem facetious anymore. They seemed lost. Lost to him anyway. "You have a lot to learn about loneliness."

"Do I?"

He remembered her story, feeling stupid for having said something so cruel. "Perhaps not. I'm sorry."

A gold fairy landed on Jane's shoulder, then another on her arm. "Well at least we know how my kiss made you feel," Peter said.

She shrugged. "It was all right."

"I'd find that easier to believe if you could say it without that grin on your face."

Jane blushed. Even in the dimness Peter could see it. Grateful it was her turn, he reached out a hand to help her up. "C'mon, we'd better get on our way."

When they stood, Peter tried to release Jane's hand, but she didn't let go. She held fast, her eyes penetrating. "Thank you for bringing me here. For showing me the fairies."

Peter gulped. "You're welcome."

"And thanks for the kiss."

He nodded once. "You've very welcome."

She let go, and Peter turned around, ready to venture out. In the distance, he caught sight of a pair of eyes watching them from Brim Lake. Though far from the creature, Peter could tell it watched with a glare. "C'mon, Jane. We've got to get out of here. Now."

Under a White Moon

A warm rush swelled in Peter's chest, leaving behind an assured comfort. He knew that feeling.

"I think the moon will be white when we reach Winter Quarter," he said.

"What makes you think that?" Jane asked. They had paused for another drink.

"How do you feel?" he asked her.

Jane stood up from the bank of the river where they'd stopped. She placed her hands on her hips and looked at their surroundings. The eternal dusk couldn't mask her appeal. Peter found himself watching her a little too closely. One kiss. No more. That's it. He tried to force his eyes away and distracted himself with having a drink as well.

"Wow," she said. "I feel calm. Like everything is going to be okay. Forever. It feels amazing. What is it?"

"It's the best feeling in existence," Peter said.

"What's that?"

"How would you describe it?"

Jane closed her eyes and pondered. Peter finished drinking and went through his pack merely to avoid staring at her.

"Peaceful."

Peter smiled at her, amazed by how naturally she came to understand the mysteries of this place. "That's it. Peace is the best feeling in the world. C'mon. The white moon is truly stunning."

They finally reached the dark of Winter Quarter, which almost seemed lighter than dusk given the white moon. It appeared to be ten times or so larger than the moon on Earth, and when it shone white, glowed brighter than anything that could be found on the Mother Land.

Peter's foot sunk into a deep blanket of snow, producing a crunching sound.

Jane let out a laugh. "I haven't seen this much snow since I was a child in New Jersey." She took off and ran through it, finally dropping onto her back and swinging her arms and legs to make a snow angel.

"You're just like one of the children."

She giggled some more. "Peter, why don't you live here with the Lost Boys? Think of it. Sledding every day."

He sat down near her, allowing her to enjoy the experience of Never snow at her leisure. Unlike Earth's snow, it never melted, never froze, never disappeared, never changed. Or so it seemed. Peter spotted something on a distant hill. "Looks like we're not the only ones enjoying the white moon."

Jane sat up and turned to see where Peter looked.

"The Lost Boys," Jane said. She got up, slipping once or twice, but never deterred, and ran to them.

"Jane!" someone shouted. Peter couldn't tell who. Then he heard Charlie's voice, followed by Misty's. "Jane! Jane!" they all called.

No one seemed as excited to see Peter.

"Come sledding with us!"

"I'm coming," Jane yelled. "Wait for me."

They didn't wait. Several of them jumped onto the sled—an old-fashioned toboggan, actually—and began to race down the steep hill. Peter smiled. They must have felt it as well: the peace encompassing Neverland. Sledding under the white moon became tradition long ago.

Jane joined the kids at the bottom of the hill, toppling onto the sled and snow in a heap. Peter relaxed on his way up the hill, grateful the whole group was now gathered together.

"Hi, Bryson." Peter greeted Bryson and Karl at the top of the hill while Jane and the others climbed back up. The boys smiled at him, and Karl slapped his shoulder. A little peace in Neverland brought them all together. It never failed.

"Who wants to go down next?" Jane asked, breathless.

"There's another sled too," Bryson said. "Really, we could all pile in and go if we wanted to."

"I call riding with Jane," Charlie said, jumping up and down with his hand in the air.

Jane looked to Peter. "Coming?" she asked, a hopeful note in her voice. "Oh, why not?"

Peter, Simon, Misty, Frank, and Bryson all crammed into one toboggan. Jane, Charlie, Karl, Preston and Timothy piled up in the other.

"Race you!" Charlie yelled.

Bryson used his hands to shove them to a start, and Karl got the others going. With Bryson and Peter in the same sled, Jane and her brood didn't stand a chance. Peter allowed himself the thrill of the ride, savoring the easiness, the lack of worry, and just accepting the rush downward, the wind in his hair, and the final crash at the bottom. The sled tipped, throwing them all out. Jane's sled crashed into theirs and their bodies littered the white snow.

"This is incredible," Jane said. "We don't even have coats on, and I barely feel the cold."

"Let's go again," Charlie said.

"And after that let's play a game," Misty said.

"Like what?" Peter asked.

"Like 'Under a White Moon.'"

"Yeah, let's play that," Charlie said. "C'mon Jane. Let's go down one more time before we play the game." He looked to Peter. "Then can we have a sleepover?"

Cheers erupted from the crowd, and Peter couldn't help but laugh at their childish excitement. Sleepovers only happened in Winter Quarter, where the darkness invited them all to shut their eyes at the same time.

"Can we light a fire too?"

"Yes, yes, let's do it all," Peter agreed.

After switching up the passengers a bit, they all took another trip down the hill. Once at the bottom, they gathered in a circle. Karl cleared away some snow and placed some dry kindling and branches in the clearing. Peter sprinkled some fairy dust to help balance the temperature and dry out the wood. Using a lighter, Karl got the fire going with ease, especially with Preston using Peter's journal to fan the flame.

"How do you play 'Under a White Moon'?" Jane asked.

"Easy," Misty said. "Sometimes you lie and sometimes you tell the truth."

"Yeah," Simon said. "You could say something like 'I once ate fish under a white moon.' And the rest of us would try to guess if you really did or not. We vote on it, and if more of us guess the right answer, you don't get any points. But if we guess the wrong answer, you get a point."

"And let me guess," Jane said, sitting cross-legged right on top of the snow. It didn't even leave wet marks on her pants. "The person with the most points wins?"

"How did you know?" Charlie asked.

Jane shrugged. "Lucky guess."

"I'll go first," Misty said. "I once found a nickel under a white moon."

They took turns in a circle, Peter simply happy to watch until it was Jane's turn.

"I once kissed Peter under a white moon," Jane said.

Peter jerked his head toward her, sensing the peace seeping away. Her words held such power over him.

"True!" Misty said with delight.

"False," Charlie said. "Jane would never kiss Peter."

Not sure whether to be offended or ashamed, Peter glanced away from her.

The votes all came in: four saying true and four saying false. Only Peter's vote remained. He knew the answer. He'd kissed her only once, and that took place in Autumn Quarter. He would never forget. He sensed there was something more, however. Some trick.

"False," Peter said.

Jane sat a couple spaces away, only Misty and Charlie between them. She got up on her knees and came at him. Shocked, Peter froze while she leaned in and planted a kiss on his cheek.

"Gotcha!" she said. "That's true. Or it is now, anyway."

The children got a kick out of this. Peter, however, felt strangely exposed and only further confused. Had it all been a joke? Did she want to keep kissing him?

They went around the circle again, Peter only watching as the rest of them played. In the end, Jane won. It seemed Jane was winning everything: the game, the Lost Boys, Neverland, Peter. He had to stop thinking like that.

"All right, who wants to get ready to head back?" Peter asked.

"What about the sleepover?" Bryson asked.

Peter didn't feel tired. He knew that most of them probably didn't feel tired.

Jane yawned and stretched her arms, hands in tight fists. "I could sleep," she said.

"Maybe we should get back to Hollow Tree Wood before anyone goes to sleep. We really shouldn't all sleep at the same time," Peter said, thinking of how the pirates were back, and how close they all were to Autumn Quarter and the mermaids.

"C'mon, Peter. It will be fine. It's a white moon. What could happen?" Timothy said.

Peter didn't lack imagination. He could think of several ways to answer that question.

"Please, Peter?" This plea came from Jane.

"Oh, all right. I'm not tired, so I can stay awake and watch out for pirates," Peter said.

"What about natives?" Jane asked.

Everyone stared at Jane. Probably only Peter knew to what she referred. He never spoke of it, and none of the current Lost Boys had been around during that period of Neverland's history.

"There are no Native Americans in Neverland anymore," Peter explained.

"Where did they go?"

"Home," Peter said quietly.

The soft chatter of children who almost never grew sleepy filled Peter's ears. He sat near the fire, deterring the heat of the flame and the cold of the snow with a little fairy dust. Exercise was enough to keep them warm in this climate, but without it, they'd catch a chill. He'd given a bit to everyone and settled down to stare at the fire, hoping it might burn away his admiration for Jane. Fat chance—another phrase from Neverland. He smiled, thinking of how he'd have to explain that to Jane.

The white moon blared down at him. He thought to ask it a question. For example, how could he ever get out of this place? When would he?

How did Jane feel about him? He looked toward her, quiet now as she lay next to Charlie. They all seemed to be settling. He couldn't help feeling a little tired himself, seeing them all resting. The white moon would protect them. It was perhaps the only thing that could.

Peter lay on his back, placing his hands beneath his head and trying to let go of all the worry so that the moon, or rather, the fairy queen, could influence him. He craved feeling peaceful. But knowing the craving alone wouldn't bring it, he aimed for acceptance. All was simply as it was. He could sleep. Rest his mind. And maybe his troubles would be clearer when he woke.

MERMAIDS

*P*eter jolted awake, his clothes inexplicably damp. Had he been sweating? It didn't seem possible. Sweating in Neverland occurred with greater rarity than nearly any other normal human body function, especially in Winter Quarter.

Peter tried to shake off a premonition that there was reason for alarm. Disoriented, he looked around, noticing a strange hue reflecting off the snow. What had he dreamed? The memory faded, slipping from his grasp. He groped for it, frantically. Darkness. Not a dark room. A dark night. A dark sky. No, dark water. Dark water. The memory came closer; he continued to search. It opened piece by piece: splashing, moonlight, arms above the water, chanting mermaids, JANE!

Peter glanced to her spot near Charlie, and Jane was not there.

Peter got up, kicking Bryson in the process.

"Man, I was sleeping," Bryson grumbled.

"Bryson, wake the others. We've got to get back to camp. Jane's missing."

"Maybe she just went for a walk." He looked to the sky. Pointing, he said, "Peter, look."

The glow about them was no longer the clear light of the white moon. This moon appeared to be on fire. "Get them up," Peter ordered. "I'll meet you back at camp."

"Where are you going?" Bryson asked.

Peter knew if he told the truth, they may argue to come with him, which wouldn't help. When visiting the mermaids, one was a crowd, let alone two. Forget about the whole group of them. "Just go. I'll be back as soon as I find Jane."

Without another word, Peter reached for a bit of gold dust from his pocket. He doubted even that could dampen his fear, but it would make him fly. He lifted off, barely hearing the groggy moans of all the Lost Boys as Bryson woke them one by one. The moon lit the way, creating an orange glow over everything below him. From the air, he could already see Brim Lake. The atmosphere lightened some as he headed back into Autumn Quarter.

Feeling a bit disoriented—a result from traveling from night into dusk rather than the other way around—Peter swayed in the air, the dizziness threatening to force him to the ground. Giving in, he descended, smacking into a tree and falling the rest of the way. Peter stood and wavered like a drunken man, but managed to keep moving, eventually able to run. His bare feet stomped hard across the forest floor, barely touching the colorful leaves that littered the ground. He ran, fists pumping, heart drumming.

"Jane," he whispered. "Where are you, Jane?"

His ears alerted him to a loud humming. He knew that sound, hated that sound. As he got closer, he also heard splashing and then a faint cry. Was she calling his name? Or screaming?

"Jane!" Peter yelled.

The trees finally cleared, revealing Brim Lake, an oval of water surrounded by giant trees resembling redwoods. Darkness seemed to engulf him. Without the light of the moon—regardless of color—Autumn Quarter was nearly as dark as where he'd just been. Stillness pierced the air. Nothing but still, clear water stared back at him. Even his own reflection evaded him in the darkness.

The sound of splashing returned, and the lake revealed a pair of flailing arms.

"Jane!" Peter yelled.

Her head popped up, and out came the desperate cry again. Peter thought he heard his name, even amid the gurgling.

He dove in, disregarding any thought of consequences and the circle of angry, scaly mermaids rising around Jane, each pointing a spear in her direction. He could hear them even beneath the surface of the water. They chanted, *"O eem may mo ma yah! I eem may mo vee si? O eem may mo ma YAH!"*

Peter burst out of the water. "Stop!" he cried. "She's with me."

One of the mermaids glanced in his direction, gave him a look of defiance and turned back to their target. It never ceased to amaze Peter how ugly they were. Glancing at the back of a mermaid could be deceiving. But when one of the creatures faced him, Peter not only had a sinister being to deal with, but an overpowering sense of dread. Staring at a Never mermaid was like looking at one of the scary masks made for Halloween— half old woman and half monster, or some other bizarre mix that Peter had never been able to describe. Scales crawled halfway up their face and what human-like skin they had was wrinkly, probably from the constant exposure to water. Peter reminded himself to breathe and fought the fear crawling up his chest.

"Jane, listen to me."

"Peter? Peter, they're drowning me. One of them has my legs."

"Jane, listen to me." He stopped swimming outside the circle and treaded in place. "Jane, I'm going to come and help you."

"Peter, please!"

Nearly overcome by her plea, Peter fought the urge to rush in and rescue. She had to understand first. "Jane, listen."

"I'm listening!"

"You're going to have to kill one of them."

"What?" she screamed. "They're all armed."

"I'm going to come in the circle and take out the one at your feet. You're going to have to kill one of the others. It's the only way they'll let you go."

One of the mermaids turned her face toward Peter and hissed, her snake-like tongue emerging and coming too close to his face. She spoke to him. *"Ya way si fay mo kee. Peetah Pahn."* (This is not your fight.)

Peter glared at her and dove into the water once more, feeling his way through the circle and to Jane's feet. He wrapped his arm around the mermaid's head, squeezing her neck. Her fin-hands pulled and slapped at his arm, her strength beyond belief. Peter held fast, despite the abuse and the fact that this creature was nearly the same size as he was and far stronger. Using his other arm, he blocked her gills, three slits across her middle. She fought him, wrapping her arms around his waist now and trying to fight her way free. Jane's desperate attempt to free herself shoved them backward, and Peter lost his grip on the mermaid, who went for Jane once more. Peter grabbed her tail and yanked her back, punching her in the jaw and taking her in the death lock again. He held fast, using both his legs now, focusing on cutting off the blood supply at her neck and the air supply through her gills. She panicked and squirmed until she grew weaker and weaker. Peter knew it would only take a moment longer, but he needed air.

He heard a commotion above and glanced up, trying to see Jane in the darkness. A muffled scream sounded from Jane's direction. He turned his attention once more to the yellow-haired mermaid he struggled with and yanked hard on her neck. She went limp in Peter's arms.

After letting her go, Peter kicked his way to the surface, his chest feeling like it would explode any second if he didn't get some air. Emerging and gasping for breath, Peter saw that Jane fought for a spear. He knew the owner would not let go easily. The other mermaids surrounded them and poked at Jane. She cried out in pain, adding to it a scream of determination as she ripped the spear from the mermaid's hands and tried to stab her.

Jane had most likely been aiming for her heart, but mermaids didn't have hearts, at least not hearts in the way that humans did, with ventricles and chambers.

"It's too dull," Peter shouted. "Try a blow to the head."

"Why can't you help me!" Jane screamed at Peter.

Peter bowed his head as Jane attempted to hit the mermaid hard enough to cause fatal damage.

"Peter!" a voice called from the woods.

Peter turned around in the water to find Karl and Bryson running to their aid.

"No, stay back," Peter yelled, waving a hand as if pushing them away.

They stopped at the edge of the lake and began yelling at Jane. "Hit her harder," Karl yelled.

"Take her out, Jane," Bryson said.

Peter dove back into the water hoping to help hold the mermaid still or instruct Jane on how to block the gills, but two mermaids grabbed his arms and pulled him out.

"*Key es mi no fey wel li,*" one of them said. (You've done enough.)

Karl jumped into the water. Peter could tell Bryson was deliberating, but he soon jumped in as well.

"No, Bryson! Karl, get out of the water!" Peter yelled at them.

The mermaids began communicating with each other. Jane had sole possession of the spear and smacked the mermaid one last time. The creature's eyes rolled back, and she sank into the deep. The mermaids restraining Peter let go, and all the mermaids splashed into the lake and swam away. Karl and Bryson paused in their swim.

"Is she okay?" Karl asked.

Peter looked at Jane. She shivered, and tears streamed down her horror-struck face. Peter wanted to rush over to her and comfort her. Something held him back. He felt responsible, and the guilt kept him from answering the desires of his heart.

"Peter, is she going to die?" Jane asked.

"Probably." Peter paused to breathe some more. His lungs burned, and talking was difficult.

"I thought mermaids were supposed to be beautiful," Jane said. "That was so scary."

Peter grabbed his side, a stabbing pain adding another reason to slow down and concentrate on deep, slow breaths. "Just another exaggeration of Neverland characteristic."

Jane cried harder and appeared to be struggling to tread water. Without thinking, Peter swam to her and enfolded her in a tight embrace. "Shhhhh." She resisted his hold on her, looking all around them, still paranoid, and she trembled wildly, sobbing and gasping as she tried to push him away.

"Shhhhh," he said again, not having a clue what else to say to settle her down. "Hey, hey, hey, listen to me." He let go of her torso and grabbed her chin, forcing her to look in his eyes. "Hey, you did it. It's over now. Let's swim back to shore. Get Karl and Bryson back to the Hollow Tree Wood."

"What's over now? Why did I have to kill one of them? Why wouldn't you help me?" Tears still streamed from her eyes, and her lips trembled. The sight of her renewed Peter's shame. Jane's hair clung to her forehead and the sides of her face. Peter remembered the first time he'd killed a mermaid, how traumatic it had been. But after a moment, relief flooded him, replacing the remorse for the most part. Jane didn't have to worry about them anymore.

"Shhhhhh. I'll tell you when you stop crying. That way you'll actually hear me."

She kept looking around them, watching for an expected attack that Peter knew would never come.

Peter grasped her arms and shook, hoping she'd hear him. "They'll never bother you again. You'll never need to worry about them again. When mermaids capture someone, they put them through a test. See how strong they are." Peter wiped a tear off her check with his thumb. "You passed. If you die first, you lose. But if you kill one of them first, they surrender. They come to respect and fear you." He left out that they got a little touchy again if they thought you didn't hold up your end of an alliance.

Peter waited for her to respond. He hoped she would take this news well. It was fortunate in the end that she'd faced them already. He'd never need to worry about Jane and the mermaids now. Leaving would be that much easier. The somber look on her face told him she didn't quite see it like that yet. "It's okay to be afraid," Peter said. "I'm afraid of a bunch of stupid pirates."

Finally, she grinned, but the smile seemed forced. "They'll never try to hurt me again? No matter what?" Jane asked.

Peter nodded.

"Even though I'm a girl?"

"Yes. Respect is equally earned for girls and boys when it comes to mermaids." He only described what he'd barely learned in his and Jane's recent encounter with the creatures. If they'd been determined to kill her because Jane was female, they wouldn't have retreated so soon.

"I don't even remember how I got here."

"They probably put a charm over you. They can lure you through song or through a dream. Either way, it puts you in a trance." He remembered the dream that had woken him, grateful for the warning, wherever it had come from. Dreams in Neverland operated under different rules than on Earth. They often held symbolic meaning. He'd learned to pay attention.

Jane's legs kicked against Peter's as the two of them worked to stay above water. She'd resisted his arms before, and Peter didn't have enough courage to try an embrace again. Not yet, although the thought was crossing his mind. He started to shiver for the first time since he'd brought Jane to Neverland. The shaking seemed to result from a combination of the water and the nerves pestering him. Somehow her pushing him away had erased the closeness they'd been experimenting with and left him as flabbergasted as when they'd first met.

"Do you know what they were saying?" Jane asked. She looked puzzled still, as if the haze of the charm lingered.

"Yes. I've known how to communicate with them for ages. Mostly they were chanting war cries. But one made it clear that I wasn't to help you."

"Can we get out of the water?" Jane asked.

Peter reached into his pocket and pulled out a fistful of fairy dust. Some of it fell into the water and began floating away. Peter sprinkled the rest on top of Jane and himself. He grabbed hold of her hand and pulled her out of the water. They lifted into the air and flew to a large rock near Karl and Bryson.

"Are you okay, Jane?" Bryson asked.

"That was an amazing hit," Karl said.

"Karl! Take Bryson back to the others. Let them know we're all okay," Peter said.

Karl and Bryson left, and Jane sat down on the rock.

"I can't believe I ever had an alliance with them," Peter muttered.

"The mermaids? You had an alliance with them?" Her tone displayed her horror at such a thought.

"They can be useful. Especially for keeping things hidden."

"What things?"

"Never mind. Let's get you out of here and head back home."

Before they could turn to leave, Jane grew unnervingly quiet. She sat on the rock with her arms around her legs, as if she had no intention of leaving. She stared at the lake. "Peter, how do you get back to Earth?"

This struck him like a blast of Never lightning, and he couldn't quite say the reason. Did he fear to lose her for the sake of Neverland and his plans? Or did he fear to lose her for the simple fact that he'd grown so fond? He searched his heart, finding a sadness there. Light gray. That's how he felt about the idea of Jane leaving, and the sadness was more because he didn't want to be without her. What in the Neverland stars was he going to do now?

"Let's get out of here. Then I'll show you."

So much for another kiss. Jane had almost died, two mermaids had lost their lives, and Jane seemed to be thinking about leaving Neverland. His plan was crumbling, and he didn't have enough time left on Earth to find someone else. If Jane left, he would have to stay. Forever. If Jane left, he'd have to stay forever . . . without her.

SAYING GOOD-BYE

*B*ack in Winter Quarter, Peter led Jane through the forest of Never
Pointed trees, beyond several mountain peaks and up a steep, rocky
incline. Bare of snow, the rocks gathered and stretched upward. When
Peter and Jane reached the top, Peter looked down into the black hole surrounded by the rocks on which they stood.

Jane turned and took in the surrounding view, however. Peter watched
her as she observed: Autumn Quarter with all its color, Spring Quarter
with its blossoms and meadows. When her eyes fell on Brim Lake, she
shuddered and turned to face him.

"Where are we?"

"This is the falling place."

"The what?"

He nodded to the enormous opening near their feet. She glanced at it
and gasped, backing away.

"It's okay. There's nothing to hurt you in there."

"Except sharp rocks and a death landing."

"There is no landing. No bottom. And don't worry about the rocks.
They can't hurt you once you fall in. The suction is strong and precise. It's
like traveling through a tube, really."

She gaped at him, then investigated the hole. "This is how you get
back?"

"It's one of the ways. You can always fly back if you have the fairy dust
you need and know how to get to the worm hole. But here, you don't need
anything. You're sucked into a tube that leads to another wormhole. It

sucks you safely all the way back to Earth and spits you out near the coast of Bangkok."

"Thailand? And how do I get home from there?"

Peter shrugged.

"What home?" she asked, still studying that great, black space. "It's not like I have anywhere in particular to go."

Her clothes appeared to be soaked through still. "Are you cold?" Peter asked.

"Yeah, a little."

He reached into his pack and pulled out the fairy dust. Rather than extract some he handed her the black velvet pouch. "Here," he said. "Take this. Use some to keep yourself warm. You can save the rest just in case. That way you can go back to the train station and start over. Pretend like none of this ever happened."

She faced him. "I could never do that. I'll always cherish this place. I'm glad you brought me, Peter."

Cherish it as in stay and cherish it, or cherish it in her memory? Peter couldn't bring himself to ask out loud. Perhaps he didn't want to know the answer, just in case it wasn't favorable. Time would tell. Then again, here on Neverland, time didn't exist. They could have millions of moments and experiences before she decided to leave. He shook his head, trying to blot out those thoughts. Wasn't he the one who was supposed to be planning to leave? What had she done to him?

"What is it?" she asked.

"Nothing, I just . . . We should get back."

"I've never met anyone in an eternal world who was always in such a hurry."

He smiled at her. "Have you met anyone else in any eternal worlds?"

"Nope."

"All right then. Hold your tongue."

She placed her fingers on his bare arm. Peter looked down at her hand, resisting his desire to take it. Instead, he focused on this instance, this flicker of touch, her skin on his.

"Peter, I never thanked you for coming to my aid. I can't imagine what would have happened to me if you hadn't come."

Soaking up her gaze, the feel of her hand on his arm, Peter held still. "You're welcome."

She gave his arm a gentle squeeze and turned to descend the mountain.

It took Peter a moment to recover his senses, as if she hadn't moved at all, or perhaps the disappointment of her absence was what stupefied him. "Jane, wait. If we go down this way, we'll come out near Hollow Tree Wood."

"Really? You live this close to the falling place?"

Perhaps it had been foolish to reveal that. "Yes."

"Lead the way then."

Peter reached for her hand. "Help you down?" He knew she didn't need the help, and he knew she probably knew it. He also knew it seemed agony to not have her hand in his.

Jane stared at his hand before looking him in the eye and finally accepting his offer.

They descended the mountain hand in hand, and when they reached the bottom, Jane let go. Peter watched the disconnection, staggered by the loss, and placed his hands in his pockets.

"Jane! I see Jane!" Charlie's voice rang out through the air. The sound of crunching snow ended, replaced by the cadences of Never song birds. The Never Pointed trees were now gone, and the Hollow Tree Wood had begun. The world of endless dawn greeted them, shutting out the dark of winter.

Charlie ran through the trees, and Jane bent down to receive him. She lifted him and swung him around in a few circles until she wrapped her arms around him. Peter couldn't help the jealousy. She had let go of him and now smothered Charlie in hugs and kisses. He watched them over his shoulder and continued into their camp.

"Look who's back," Bryson said.

"What's this?" Peter asked.

"We're having school. Karl's teaching us how to make ropes and tie knots," Frank said.

"He says that on Earth people have to use ropes and knots when they climb rocks!" Timothy said. "He says it's because the gravity pull is a hundred times stronger than it is here."

"Fantastic," Peter said, smiling at the boy's enthusiasm. "Thanks for taking care of everyone, Bryson."

He nodded, glowing with pride.

"How's Jane?" Misty asked.

"Safe," Peter mustered, sitting on a tree stump. He looked to the sky, feeling again the relief this fact brought him.

Preston approached him from behind. "Peter, can I talk to you?"

Peter glanced at his face, sensing leeriness in his expression.

"Sure, what is it?" Peter asked.

"Alone?"

He couldn't remember Preston ever asking to speak with him alone. Peter mentally searched for possible reasons Preston wanted to speak alone now. One reason came to mind. Could he be ready to leave them as well?

"Sure, let's go into my tree," Peter said.

Preston led the way, and Peter watched him from behind, looking for telltale signs of nervousness, thinking perhaps they would give something away. But once the door closed, Preston turned to face Peter and began to tell all, leaving little to Peter's imagination and confirming his suspicion.

"Peter, I'd like to go back. I like it here, and I'm grateful for everything you've done for me, but I'm ready to face the world again."

"I know. I imagine you've always been ready."

Preston stood tall, taller than Peter thought possible for one so young. And brave—Peter couldn't remember anyone as brave as this child standing before him.

"What do you remember about your life there or how you came here?"

"I think I remember my mother. She and I were walking down a sidewalk. She had heels on and a green skirt."

"Do you remember what year it was?"

"Year?"

Did this mean he had no recollection of time on Earth?

"Never mind. What happened?"

"I think somebody took me."

"Like a stranger? Were you kidnapped?"

"I'm not sure."

"Okay. Do you remember how you got here?"

Peter remembered. He just wanted to see if Preston did.

"The Tally Man brought me. I think."

"Indeed. Well done, Preston. That is a lot to remember. More memories may come back as you keep thinking of the Mother Land. No need to rush. Let's talk often, and I'll help prepare you for the journey." Peter knew the most difficult thing to explain would be time, and how his mother might be long gone by now.

"I want to go now."

Taken aback, Peter stared until ready to continue the conversation he'd been prepared to let rest. "Right now?" Peter asked.

"Yes," the boy answered.

"Why?"

He hung his head. "I think I'll lose courage if I wait."

"I see." Peter knew it went like that sometimes. Courage or desire would waver. "I didn't want to tell you this so soon, but things will be different than you remember. Things will have changed drastically. People will be older, perhaps some of them will have even passed on."

"Peter, I'm not an idiot."

Peter let out a sigh of relieved laughter. "No, I didn't think so. What do you plan to do once you get back?"

"Find a police officer and tell him that I can't find my mom."

"That sounds like a good plan. Growing up can be hard."

"I know, Peter. And I'm ready."

"Would you like to say good-bye to the others?"

At this, a tear formed at the corner of the boy's eye. He shook his head. "I don't want them to try to talk me out of it."

"What about Jane?"

"I only want you, Peter. Will you help me find the wormhole?"

"I think I can do a little better than that. I'll take you back myself."

Preston beamed. "Will you?"

"Absolutely. Let's tell the others we're taking a walk to find the Tally Man. Just the two of us."

After explaining they were venturing into the wood looking for the Tally Man, Peter and Preston walked away from camp. In the thick of the trees, Peter took out some fairy dust and sprinkled it on them both. Part of him wanted to convince Preston to wait, to prepare a little more. But knowing Preston, he'd probably been preparing for ages and just hadn't let anyone know.

"Ready?" Peter asked.

Preston nodded.

"Let's go then."

They lifted off and soared above the hollow trees, traveling first toward Summer Quarter to avoid being seen by the others. Peter led Preston high into the atmosphere and straight to the wormhole. He couldn't tell by Preston's expression whether he found it thrilling or frightening. Such a stone-faced boy. Even when they exited the wormhole, passed into the Milky Way and approached Earth—currently a blue mass covered in swirls of clouds—Preston gave nothing away.

The sun shone bright in London, alerting Peter to their need to stay clear of airplanes and keep out of sight until they landed. Locating a high-rise Peter knew had easy access from the roof, Peter and the Lost Boy found their footing. They entered the building through an unlocked door. After descending a short staircase, Peter looked both ways and led Preston to an elevator.

Preston never seemed to get nervous until several people got on the elevator, eyeing his shabby appearance. "It's okay," Peter whispered. "Everything is going to work out."

Once on the ground floor, Peter led Preston through a lobby with marble floors and out a rotating door that fascinated the Lost Boy. Preston went around in a few circles before exiting.

The noise on the street thrilled Peter. He loved London in the morning. Cars honked, and people sped in both directions all around them, conversing with one another or looking at their phones. Peter spotted a police officer and nudged Preston. "Look." He pointed to a woman sitting in a car across the street. Dressed in full uniform, including a black-and-white checkered hat and a bright-yellow vest, the woman appeared to be writing out a ticket. Peter thanked the Neverland stars they'd found a female officer first. He thought that would somehow be easier for Preston.

"I guess this is good-bye," Preston said.

Peter looked down at the boy. Preston's eyes remained focused on his destination, the woman across the street.

"Remember to look both ways before crossing."

"This place is different from Neverland, isn't it?" Preston glanced at Peter.

"Very. In good ways and in some not so pleasant ways." Peter gestured to the commotion around them. "But you'll be fine. You're going to have an amazing childhood. An amazing life."

"Thanks, Peter." The boy threw his arms around Peter's waist, and Peter accepted the hug, which Preston did not prolong. He let go and, after checking for traffic, began crossing the street. Knowing his cover could be blown if the woman saw him, Peter turned and walked away, back into the building, up the elevator, out the door at the roof, and up into the sky, never looking back until Neverland came into view. More than missing Preston, Peter envied him. As crowded and noisy as London could be, it was the place Peter longed for more than any other.

PIRATE ATTACK

The Never moon glowed bright, a lime green. Not fazed in the slightest by this, Peter continued to Spring Quarter, landing near the bottom of the mountain where he and Jane had held hands before. When he entered Hollow Tree Wood, he could feel it. Danger. It almost had a smell on Neverland. Or perhaps the pirates smelled so foul they personified danger with their scent. Rotten milk and body odor with a smattering of alcohol. That's what danger smelled like to Peter. His heart quickened, an onslaught of fears gripping his mind. Had the Lost Boys been harmed? Had anyone been kidnapped? What about Jane?

Peter sped into their ramshackle camp, finding everything displaced, much of it destroyed. The seats around the campfire lay strewn about; Bryson's cooking station had been overturned; destroyed tree branches hung by their final woody threads. Peter ran to the open door of the nearest hollow tree.

"Jane? Bryson? Timothy? Misty? Anyone?"

He tore apart Misty's tree, flinging clothes and bedding, all of which had been strewn in heaps around her floor. Peter checked the next natural dwelling, and the next—each one as messy and altered as the one before. Then he remembered the trapdoor in his own abode and the one in the makeshift hospital. He checked his tree first, finding only his sketchbooks, journals and stacks of fairy dust organized by color on the table, the black in a sealed bag.

"Where could they be?" Peter murmured. He ran up the ladder of his cellar and closed the trap door. Making his way to the hospital, he heard a commotion.

"Peter, is that you?" came a voice from inside the sick tree.

"Bryson? Oh, thank the Neverland stars."

Bryson stood at the door, peering out. "It's okay, everyone. It's only Peter," Bryson said.

They filed out of the tree, and Peter took in every face, but he still needed to see one in particular to ease his mind. Finally, Jane came out with Charlie attached to her hip. Peter fought the urge to reach for her. He inspected their faces, looking for any bruises or cuts, any brandings or cut-off hair. They all looked well enough, perhaps even relieved to see him. "What happened?"

"Pirates. We could smell them coming so we hid in the shelter," Frank said, holding his suit jacket in his arm rather than wearing it. He even went without his hat.

"Typical," Peter said, huffing at the pirates' stupidity. Couldn't they bathe before attacking? Not that he wanted them to—it was nice to be alerted.

"It still smells," Misty said.

"Agreed," Jane added, her face scrunched up in reaction to the odor.

"It may smell for quite a while," Peter said. "Something that strong doesn't dissipate easily."

Peter heard someone ticking their tongue in mock disappointment. He jerked around to see Sven, knife in hand whittling a stick. "Peter, Peter, Peter." He dropped the stick and turned to them, a wicked glint in his eye. Peter fought the urge to run; he had to face him, had to be brave.

"Hold on, Sven." Peter put his hands up.

"Attack!" The voice came from behind Peter. He turned to see Jack Raven, Sven's first mate. He was an Asian man who wore a constant smile and an eye patch he didn't need. Peter knew the man only wore the accessory when the pirates were plundering and the like. Jack Raven plucked Timothy off the ground, swooping his arm around the boy's chest.

"Wait, wait, wait, wait," Peter pleaded. He couldn't bear to see any of the Lost Boys in pirate hands.

Out from the trees stepped Bob, a short, fat pirate who posed little threat, mostly because he could never catch any of them. He waddled straight up to Jane and attempted to force Charlie from her arms. Jane held tight, resisting while Charlie began to cry. She let him go when the man produced a pistol.

"Shhhh, don't cry, Charlie," she said. "Everything will be okay."

Larry and Harry came out as well, twins whom Peter had never seen apart. One of them grabbed the two closest to him—Simon and Frank—while the other walked across camp to retrieve Misty, who looked as though she might run.

"Enough!" Peter shouted. "Stop this. I'm the one you're after. Let them go, and I'll come back to the cliffs with you."

Russa came out, and a chill ran up Peter's spine. His courage wavered. Next to Sven, Russa scared Peter the most. Messy dreadlocks came to his knees. They held bits and pieces of glass and razor blades, and he would use them to whip captors if they did anything to displease him. Peter's wounds from his last capture seemed to throb. Russa was the only pirate Peter had never seen smile. In fact, he felt confident the man held loyalties to no one and would throw Sven out if he ever got the chance. He'd probably failed so far at swaying the others against him because Sven had never hesitated to kill anyone disloyal to him. Russa caught Bryson in a headlock and pulled tighter until Bryson stopped shuffling his feet. Eerie came out last. Creepy and masochistic, the thin man had scars all over his face, chest and arms. He had short, red hair, a mustache, and goatee.

"Where are the others?" Sven asked. "That wild one and . . . aren't there a couple others missing?"

Peter didn't answer.

"Answer me!"

Peter held up his hands. "Just calm down, Sven." His body held enough fairy dust to escape, but most of the others were already bound. He and Jane could get away and then plan an offensive attack to rescue them. But the pirates might have enough fairy dust to chase them in the air anyway, and Peter would not leave anyone behind. Sven's tactics had proven too cruel. He'd have to use negotiation and reason.

Sven approached Jane. "And who's this? Have you brought another mother, Peter? Aren't you getting a little old for that? There are far better uses for a woman than bedtime stories and lullabies." His knife pointed at Jane's throat, Sven circled her, until turning to Peter once more. "Tell me where the others are, or I'll take her. She would fetch a pretty penny back in Bangkok."

Now that he looked closer, Peter realized Karl wasn't among them.

Retaliation would be pointless. The pirates all held weapons, and the Lost Boys had been caught off guard. This was part of the game. He'd have to find out what they wanted.

"Hold it," Peter said.

"Give us one reason why," Jack Raven answered, smiling as he clutched Timothy in one arm. The boy fidgeted and looked horrified, forcing a flare of anger in Peter.

"Where are they?" Sven asked, moving his knife closer to Jane's neck.

Peter focused all his energy on keeping cool as he watched Sven start to spin around Jane like a vulture again.

"Go on, answer." His knife got closer to her neck. "I'm getting impatient." He continued to move around her, and Jane tensed up whenever the knife brushed across her skin.

Enough waiting. Sven never played by the rules, not once in all his time as captain. Peter's shoulders slumped, and he looked to the ground. "I don't know where Karl is, but the others might. Lester has gone back to the Mother Land." He'd hoped to break it to everyone under better circumstances, but the situation called for thorough honesty. "And Preston has gone back to Earth as well."

Peter braved a glance at the Lost Boys. Frank and Timothy both shot looks of shock at Peter. Bryson looked betrayed, and Peter didn't blame him; he hadn't even told his right-hand man.

Peter searched Jane's face, hoping for a sign of what she might be feeling. Her eyes kept watch over the knife as Sven passed in front of her again. Her lips trembled, and Peter knew the truth: despite her bravery and sense of adventure, Neverland frightened her. He never should have brought her.

"And you, Peter? Where were you recently? Your age calculator has been . . . counting."

"I only took Preston back," Peter said.

Sven turned his focus to Jane. "And how did you get here?" Sven asked her. "Is she the reason you spent so much time on Earth while we were there?"

Jane looked to Peter.

"It's okay," Peter told her. "No need to keep secrets."

Sven threw his head back in laughter. "This coming from you? Peter Pan, the master of secrets?" Sven stopped laughing and looked to Peter. He smiled and began ticking his tongue again. "I see. You've brought her here to replace you, haven't you? You've been planning to escape."

Peter stood firm. "Shut up, Sven!"

Sven chuckled again. "Peter, you are too much. Does she know about this plan? Tell us, Peter, have you even told the Lost Boys?"

Peter stood firm. He glared at Sven, grit his teeth, and spat on the ground. It took all his self-control not to spit directly at Sven, who must have only guessed this truth since Peter had never spoken a word of it to him.

"Peter, is it true?" Bryson asked. "Are you planning to leave Neverland?"

"Are you done, Sven?" Peter said, disregarding Bryson's inquiry. "We all know that you came for me, so get on with it." He didn't care anymore. They could torture him until he died, but he would not see them take one of the Lost Boys and especially not Jane.

"Peter brought me here." Jane's voice began to work its magic. She sounded confident, as if she'd gained control of her fears and had a plan. Hearing it sent a rush of calm through Peter. He trusted her to say something brilliant. "He brought me here because he loves me. He asked me to stay here in Neverland. Forever. With him."

Sven finally lowered his knife, looking dumbstruck. Peter wondered what Jane was up to and if he was supposed to play along or just keep his mouth shut. Peter looked around at everyone. Misty and the Lost Boys now watched Jane with hopeful expressions, where before, several of them had shed tears at Sven's news about Peter's plans to leave.

"Well, this is unexpected, I must say. Peter has not found him a mother. He has found himself a lover." He laughed hysterically at his own pathetic attempt at poetry, and all the pirates joined in the revelry except Russa, whom Peter noticed eyed Jane with far too much derision.

"It's true," Peter said. "I've brought her here so that I can bear to stay." He kept his eyes focused on Jane's. "I won't leave Neverland. Ever. You have my word."

Sven lowered his knife and abandoned his object of prey to approach Peter. Relief flooded Peter's heart seeing him leave Jane alone. Sven brought his face within inches of Peter's and whispered coarsely in his ear. "I know your word is worth nothing, Peter. And I know how old you are. Do you know how much time you have left? How many ticks remain on the clock counting down to your eighteenth birthday? The day you waltz out of childhood forever and become one of us?"

Peter shook his head. "Not exactly."

"Well let's put it this way, Peter. One more trip to Earth, and you belong to my crew. Unless you'd rather die. I'd be happy to oblige. And we'll be watching." He pulled the device from his chest pocket and held it in front of Peter's face. "I carry it with me always."

Peter raised his eyebrows and tried to get a glimpse of the reading on his age calculator. Sven's smell began to nauseate Peter. He shoved down both the acid crawling up his esophagus and the nagging desire to plug his nose. It only worsened when Sven leaned in closer. Peter coughed, his gag reflex kicking in. "Do you know what happened to the last Lost Boy who defied me? Take a good look at Russa."

Peter looked back into Sven's cold eyes and then glanced at Russa, searching for any possible meaning in Sven's words.

"That's right, Peter." He spoke more softly now, as if he didn't want the others to know. "Recognize him? Children in Neverland aren't supposed to grow up, Peter. And yet, you have." He made that infernal ticking noise with his tongue again, slicing away at Peter's nerves until he felt as though he would come undone. "What a shame." Sven looked back at Jane. "You'd better look after her. No telling what might happen to such a prize."

A few of the pirates snickered, signaling they'd heard Sven's last remarks. Peter searched her face, but she looked so calm now.

"C'mon, men. We don't need to waste any more time here."

"Yeah, they don't even have any brandy," Harry said.

Peter watched carefully as the pirates released their prisoners, some of them dropping or shoving the Lost Boys to the ground. Jane retrieved Charlie and Misty. Peter stared after Russa, fighting for a memory, and when it came, Peter wished he'd left it alone. Those cruel eyes had once been soft, gemlike even. He once had blond hair and knobby knees and was the best climber in the history of Neverland. Cole had been his name then.

In a daze, Peter barely noticed the pirates' retreat and the Lost Boys' attempt to clean up camp under Bryson's direction.

"I think we'll need a good meal after that," Bryson said. Peter agreed. Comfort food. Lots of it. Peter hated making decisions when it came to Sven and the rest of the pirates. He could never be sure how much of a threat they posed. Sometimes they would kidnap and torture, and other times they'd disappear to the Mother Land and become too preoccupied or too drunk to come back and make good on their threats.

Jane worked to distract the youngest Lost Boy and Misty (and probably herself as well), and Peter tried to remember all that had happened, all that had been said. He'd been so pumped with emotion, he found the memories fuzzy, but he felt certain Jane had saved him and the Lost Boys. They all had heard two stories about Peter—one from Sven and one from Jane—and who could say which they'd believe? Peter reasoned that people usually believed what was more pleasant to believe. He breathed easier, until remembering his promise to Sven, the assurance that he'd remain in Neverland. Realizing the truth about Russa seemed to make it more real and necessary to keep. Peter never wanted to become a pirate. Nor did he want to remain in Neverland eternally. He had no desire to live forever anymore, but he couldn't die yet, not with all he still wanted to do: settle down, have a family of his own, see the Mother Land up close rather than from an otherworldly distance.

Jane looked at him, still smiling from something Charlie had said. Maybe, just maybe, he could tolerate it with Jane around. Keeping-me-sane-Jane, Peter mused.

A loud commotion—followed by a scream and some crying—drew Peter from Jane's pleasant gaze.

"What was that?" Bryson asked, looking at Peter.

A little boy stumbled into camp, black hair matching the dirt scuffs all over his face and arms. He looked up to see all of them and pulled away in fright, turning slightly as if debating whether to run.

"Wait," Timothy said. "Are you a Lost Boy?"

"Where am I?" the boy asked. "Who are all of you?"

Jane stood up and approached Peter. "Peter, what's going on? Who is this?"

All eyes stared back and forth between the boy and Peter. Peter's heart beat fast several times then slowed again, forcing the air from his lungs. It sped again, sucking away every attempt he made to get a deep breath. Closing his eyes, Peter succumbed. His knees buckled, and all went black.

PANIC

*P*eter opened his eyes, disoriented at first from waking up to unfamiliar surroundings. He searched for his desk and the artwork of hundreds of Lost Boys on his walls but came up empty. A buzzing sounded in his ear, and his vision blurred. His heart sped and stole the breath from him once more. Peter began taking small, quick breaths, hoping that one of them—just one—might fill his lungs with enough air to provide momentary relief.

"Hey, shhh, shhh, shhh."

Peter squinted, both blinded by the light and frustrated by the lack of focus. "Jane?" Even the small act of saying her name brought some respite.

"I'm here," she said. Peter felt her hand grasp his. The warmth of her palm made him realize how cold and tingly his outer extremities felt.

"Jane, where's the boy? What happened?"

"Shh, don't worry about it. He's fine. Bryson's taking care of him. Just relax."

Peter's vision sharpened, and his heart settled. That's when mortification struck. Bright lanterns above revealed his location: the sick tree. Jane sat at his side, still holding his hand. He squirmed away from her, backing against the wall and sitting up. He pulled the Never ginger sheets up to his neck, considering this better than hiding beneath them completely.

"Jane, please leave. I can't bear to have you see me like this." His heart began to race again.

"Oh, stop. It's not like I've never seen a panic attack before. My parents used to get them all the time when they had to stay sober long enough to go to work."

"Seriously?" The hyperventilating set in again.

"Hey, take it easy. Try to take a deep breath. You're not going to die. You're not going to run out of air. I'm not going to let anything happen to you."

Panic attacks were new to Peter, and they terrified him. But somehow, he believed Jane. She spoke with such surety. He believed her because she believed her own words. At least, she sounded like she did.

"Better?" she asked.

He nodded. "Yeah, a little."

The memory of the pirates came back to him, including the way Sven had threatened Jane's safety. Peter hugged the sheet close and fought to continue his deeper, more settled breathing. He thought of the Lost Boy. They needed so much care when they first came. He couldn't do it anymore. He'd rather die. Peter lay back down, curling into a ball. Misery threatened to consume him. He had to escape this place.

"Wanna talk about it?"

Peter glanced up at Jane, craving solitude and resisting the urge to cover his head.

Peter never answered, and Jane quieted, leaning back in her chair and folding her arms.

Occasionally, Charlie came in to see her, or Bryson checked on things. "Peter's fine," Jane would say. "No need to worry."

On one of Charlie's visits, he brought a drawing for Peter. "It's of the butterfly we saw."

"Of course it is," Jane replied. "I could never forget that."

"Peter forgets everything," Charlie said.

Peter concealed a smile. Charlie's innocent honesty proved the best medicine so far. "I do not."

"Can you leave us be for a moment, Charlie?" Jane asked.

Charlie growled in harmless frustration and exited the room, leaving his drawing in Jane's lap.

Jane watched him walk out and then turned to Peter. "How are you feeling now?"

"Steady," he said. "Like a still pond rather than a rushing stream or the crashing waves of the sea."

"What changed?"

"Nothing." Peter tasted the word on his lips, allowed the sound of it to echo throughout the vast hollow tree. He hated feeling so helpless, hated the unpredictability, and most of all, he hated having an audience when it hit—like silent lightning, illuminating his insides for all to see.

"How long have you had panic attacks?"

"You know I have no way of measuring that." Peter sat up and leaned his back against the wall. "But really just since Sven last held me captive."

"Can I get you anything?"

Peter shook his head.

Jane watched him, and all Peter could think about was how much explaining he had to do and how possible it was that she would hate him afterward.

"How old do you think you were when the anxiety started?"

He pulled his knees to his chest and hugged his shins. He'd never thought about it like that, never given it a label, and suspected Jane was reading into it too much. Then an answer flew out of his mouth. "Maybe twelve or thirteen. When I started spending more time on Earth. Every time I came back here, I'd be anxious. I'd also be distressed every time a new Lost Boy arrived." He chuckled. "It was worst when Simon and Misty came. I had no idea what to do about having a girl here."

"But she wasn't the first girl here, was she?"

"No." Peter bowed his head. "A few have come. We lost two to the mermaids. After that, I would take any girls that came straight back to Earth. But Misty came with Simon, so we decided to give her a chance." Peter smiled at the memory. "And we were so worried about the pirates knowing she was here—not to mention the mermaids—so we dressed her up like a boy for ages."

Jane laughed. "Poor girl." She studied Peter. "And Wendy? How did she get here?"

Peter rested against the wall and looked into Jane's brown eyes. "I brought her."

"Like me? Because you wanted a mother for the Lost Boys?"

Peter sighed and looked to the ceiling. "Something like that."

Jane shifted in her chair. "Tell me about the others. How do they get here?"

"It's pretty random, really. The Tally Man will sometimes bring a child he thinks needs saving. Some get here by accident. Fairies occasionally travel to Earth, and if the fairies get their dust on someone, and the recipient has the constitution to use it, usually because they're desperate to get out of a situation, they can wind up here."

"Peter, what's going to happen to them all?"

Peter examined her eyes, which looked more caramel right now, the color of tenderness. He had to admit her mood matched caramel more than the darker brown of a mischievous fairy. He didn't want to talk about the Lost Boys anymore. Guilt churned in his gut. Peter marveled at how Jane could face him with such collectedness after being threatened by pirates. The panic threatened to return, and he knew he needed to unload it all or he'd probably pass out again.

"Jane, what Sven said is true. I was planning to leave Neverland."

"I've known that all along, Peter."

His eyes widened. "What do you mean you've known all along?"

She tilted her head to the side, hands resting in her lap. "Well, maybe not all along, but not long after I got here, I knew you were up to something. You're so easy to read, Peter. Remember when we first met? And you were surprised to find out I knew you were following me? You're so obvious. You give everything away. I think you've become a Neverland fairy. The color of your emotions is just as visible as theirs."

Peter worked on processing all this. Like a pill too big for swallowing, it lingered in his mind, not quite making its way to where it belonged. "Then why are you still here?"

She shrugged. "Why not?"

The tightness in Peter's chest began to release. Jane had known all along. Freed of the burden of deceit, Peter began to share even more. "I hate it here, Jane. I've been here so long. I'm tired. I want to go back to Earth."

"Then do it."

Clearly she didn't understand. "But I can't leave them. That's why I brought you here, so that I could leave —"

"And I could stay." She spoke as if she hadn't quite worked out this detail yet. Perhaps Peter wore a convincing mask more than she let on.

"Why can't you all leave?" she asked.

"I've thought about it," Peter admitted. "That means foster homes for the Lost Boys, more trauma, separation—we could never see each other again. How could we explain that? And what about any children that wind up here after we leave? Who will take care of them?"

She leaned in closer, her eyes fixed on his. "Not . . . your . . . problem."

He allowed this thought to penetrate his mind. Wasn't it his problem? He'd be the one who knew. He'd be the one wondering about whoever found their way here, how they'd survive. Could he forget about it? Let it all go?

"It doesn't matter anymore," Peter said.

"What do you mean?"

"The pirates are after me. If I go back and . . . age . . . even a bit more, they'll kill me if I don't join them. London won't be safe. I may as well just stay."

"Peter, you're not making any sense. Sounds like fear talking anyway. Or perhaps you're just making excuses because you can't bear the thought of leaving forever."

Peter turned away from her and lay back, looking up at the ceiling, remembering how he and Lester had put in the floor and staircase for the upper room.

"Peter, I—"

"Shhhh, I'm thinking." Surely his predicament was more complicated than Jane's solution suggested.

"Peter, I think they're stronger than you give them credit for."

"Shhhh." He held a finger to her lips. Perhaps leaving was what he wanted, but there were others to think about: Bryson, Karl, Timothy, Frank, Simon, Misty, Charlie. And they kept coming. He wondered what the new boy's name was but didn't feel like bothering to ask Jane. Peter removed his finger from Jane's lips.

"Are you upset with me?" Jane asked. "I know the truth can be hard to hear."

Peter smiled. "You say that like you're right. But what if you're wrong?"

"What if I'm not?"

A sharp pain came to Peter's temple. Headaches were rare on Neverland, and Peter wondered why he'd be getting one now.

"I don't think I could just leave," he said. "Not without knowing there was someone here to take care of them. They're not ready to go back. I am. But they're not."

"Sounds like your mind is made up, Peter. That's half the battle."

He looked at her. She disagreed with him and yet she accepted him. "What will you do?" he asked. "Will you leave?" His mind began to swirl again. "*Half the battle*" was an overstatement. When he factored Jane into the equation, everything got more complex.

"Well I don't have plans to leave right now. Your problem is you worry too much." She stood and began straightening the room.

"What if we both stayed?" Perhaps he could tolerate it if he had her to steady him, but without her . . . The image of a black fairy came to mind, as did the writhing he'd seen pirates do after being given a dose of black fairy powder. It was all so confusing. He needed some medicine, something to take the edge off so he could think clearly. Peter watched Jane place some bottles in a cupboard and fluff an extra pillow. She either hadn't heard his question or was ignoring it.

"Jane, will you come with me somewhere?"

"Sure, where?"

"To see the fairies."

FAIRY HILL

"*T*his is where a good portion of the fairies congregate in Summer Quarter," Peter explained as he and Jane ascended the round-top hill that looked out over surrounding meadows and Hollow Tree Wood in the distance. "I meant to bring you here when we explored Neverland, but with the frantic fairies and the pirates being back, it must have slipped my mind."

Jane lifted her arm and reached for him. With gratitude, Peter accepted her hand and allowed her touch to comfort him. His ease around her had increased, as though her seeing him in such a state of stupor had melted the ice completely. No nerves between them. No pretense. No worries or cares. Just the warmth of her hand in his.

Jane gasped when she beheld the first group of fairies. She let go of his hand and hurried off to inspect them. Peter pulled a vial from the pocket of his T-shirt. "Let me know if you see a gold one or a pale yellow or a white."

"What are you doing?" she asked with a suspicious look on her face.

"Collecting."

"Oh, there's a white one!" Jane's excitement caused all the fairies to alter their hues a bit.

"Shhhhh," Peter urged, trying not to laugh at her enthusiasm. "Be calm. They'll come to you if they can sense you're a place of safety. A place of refuge."

"Refuge from what?"

Peter caught up to her and stood close enough that their arms were touching. "From worry, chaos, sorrow, grief, hatred, greed. Be peaceful, and the peaceful ones will come to you. Be happy, and the happy ones will come to you. Be hopeful, and the hopeful ones will come to you."

"What are we hoping for?" she asked. She looked so pleasant under the rays of the sun.

"We're hoping for peace, happiness, a spectacular fairy encounter, answers to questions, a way out, or a way to stay, safety from pirates. And we're hoping for nice treats from the Tally Man on his next visit."

Jane smiled and closed her eyes, holding out her hands as though she expected her extremities to be covered in glowing fairies when she opened her eyes. So naïve. Peter watched them flutter all around, each coming close enough to sense what she felt deep down—those masked, thick-skinned emotions, the ones fairies have no trouble sniffing out. A lime-green fairy got close, and dissatisfied, turned away. A gray fairy approached, and upon sensing Jane's prominent emotion, lightened to a gray blue. A gold fairy homed in, and Peter held his vial at the ready.

"There," he said. "Open your eyes."

Jane opened her eyes, and Peter witnessed the encounter. A gold fairy perched on Jane's bicep, fluttering its wings even though it didn't seem interested in flying away anytime soon.

"I think I know what you're feeling," Peter said, and Jane's beaming smile confirmed his suspicions. "It is one thing to be happy. It is another entirely to be happy in the company of another creature who is just as happy. Can you hold still while I extract some dust?"

Jane nodded, and Peter thought he saw the glisten of a joyful tear escaping the corner of her eye. Peter held the vial to the fairy's backside, careful not to disturb it. He quickly gave the fairy a confident squeeze, then another. The fairy turned a sulky light orange and flew away.

"Sorry about that. It had to be done," he said.

Jane smacked his arm. "I was enjoying that one."

"I'm sure you were, but we're working on a combination here. We can't just settle for joy. Do you think you could try to attract a peaceful one?"

"What do you mean by a combination?"

"When you combine certain fairy powders together, the combination can have healing properties."

"Peter, you're a chemist," Jane said.

He smiled at her. "I guess so, but I only work with fairy poop."

She laughed at him before turning and walking to the very top of the hill. "I think I need to lie down for this one."

Peter watched her sit down, then lean back on one elbow. She looked up to the sun and closed her eyes. Finally, she lay down all the way, legs out straight, hands resting atop her abdomen.

Once again, the fairies fluttered all about her, some braving a closer inspection. Peter watched with interest, knowing he'd never been one to conjure such intensely positive feelings on demand. It seemed to be Jane's niche, however. A white fairy landed on her nose.

"Careful when you open your eyes," he said. "It's staring you down."

Jane's lips moved ever so slightly, forming a tiny smile. Gradually, she opened her eyes a bit at a time.

"Watch it," Peter warned. "Try not to smile too much. Try not to let the joy take over. Just soak up the feeling of peace." He leaned down and extracted two puffs of powder from the fairy. Not appearing much altered by the intrusion, the fairy flew away without changing colors in the slightest.

"This is incredible," Jane said, sitting up and watching the fairies flit about. "What's this color mean?" she asked, pointing to a deep burgundy.

"Slothful," Peter said.

She pointed, and Peter shared what he'd learned over the years.

"Peter, why do you think those fairies were flying away when we were by the mermaids?"

"Probably just one of Sven's attempts to capture them. He does that every now and then. The fairies learn quickly though. When they see another fairy die, they remember what it was that killed them and never touch it. They were most likely fleeing from something they perceived as a trap. Pirates are so thick." Peter sat next to her and wrapped his arms around his legs, suppressing thoughts of Sven's threats. "They'll never be able to catch fairies en masse. You have to be in tune with your emotions for that, and pirates are about as emotionally plugged up as possible."

This seemed to comfort her. "How many more?" she asked. "For the remedy?"

"Just one more," Peter said. "Hope."

Her face straightened. "This is a lot of pressure. Hope has never been my greatest strength."

Peter gave her a reassuring smile and held out his hand. "Together?"

She accepted his offer, and Peter squeezed tight as he began to express his hopeful thoughts. "I hope that the pirates accidentally eat rotten shrimp for their next meal."

Jane laughed. "Are there even rotten shrimp here?"

"Doesn't matter," Peter said. "Doesn't matter if you think it's possible or not. Just say the things that you truly hope for. And yes, by the way. There are plenty of rotten shrimp on that pirate ship."

Jane gave him one last brave smile and closed her eyes. "I hope for rain so Charlie and I can jump in puddles again."

"That's it," Peter said. "I hope Preston finds a nice home and family."

"I hope for that one too," Jane added.

"I hope the new Lost Boy is getting settled."

"Me too," Jane said. "And I hope Bryson is cooking something delicious. I haven't eaten in ages."

"Food does sound good." Peter watched her expression, the way she fought for this emotion that seemed all too elusive sometimes. "I hope Jane reunites with her nanny someday."

"That would be splendid. I hope my parents can find what true happiness is."

Peter began to falter, watching the perfect, smooth skin on her face. "I hope Jane stays in Neverland with me."

As if she ignored him, Jane continued. "I hope Peter finds what he's looking for."

He'd already found it, though. "I hope Jane kisses me again soon." Peter knew the sincerity behind the hope statements mattered. He wasn't joking, or messing around, or playing with her mind.

Jane opened her eyes, and Peter was glad to see she picked up on the honesty of his statement. No more deceit.

"How is a hope different from a wish?" Jane asked.

Peter glanced at her lips. He tried to shove back the temptation, tried to remember it was hope he should be grasping for, not Jane.

"I expect hopes come to fruition more often than wishes," he said.

"I hope a hopeful fairy lands on your lips. Then you can have your hopeful kiss." She smiled at him.

"I hope I get to throw you in a stream again." Peter almost spit away the fairy that landed on his bottom lip. A light-yellow-colored fairy flapped its dainty wings. Peter had to cross his eyes to see it. "Here," Peter said, holding out the vial to Jane. "Give it a squeeze."

"I am not making that beautiful creature poop. What if I miss and it lands in your mouth?" She could barely contain her laughter.

"I hope Jane stops laughing so we can get this done," Peter said, not wanting to encourage the fairy to leave by feeling annoyed or anything else that Jane's comment might tempt him to feel. "Just do it."

"Okay, okay," she said, wiping a stray tear away. "I sure hope this works." She took the vial from him, held it at the end of the fairy and gave a squeeze.

"I hope for a bit more," Peter said, willing the fairy to remain hopeful. Jane squeezed again, and the fairy flew off, deepening in yellow but not quite making it to orange.

Jane pointed to his face. "Gross, I think some did get on your lip."

"Really?" Peter asked, feeling his mouth for traces of the silky dust.

"No chance I'm ever going to kiss those lips again now."

"Fine," Peter said. "Settle for a fairy dust combination curative?"

"What's the difference between that and a kiss?"

"None whatsoever," Peter said, smiling. "Unless, of course, it isn't a real kiss."

"Thanks for bringing me here," Jane said.

"Thanks for making a fairy poop on my lip."

"That sounds so wrong."

"Here," Peter said, holding out the vial and giving it a shake to mix up the fairy dusts. Take some of this and sprinkle it on top of your head."

"Will it still make me fly?"

"It's a surprise. Just try it."

Eyes wide and looking upward, she stood and sprinkled the concoction on her head. Peter could hardly wait to see her reaction. Her smile brightened instantly, and she lifted her arms up to steady herself; she'd have to learn to balance again.

"How does that feel?" He stood and faced her.

She pondered a moment, savoring the sensations. "It's like I'm standing on Earth again!" She spun around and let out a hearty laugh. "I feel grounded. I'd forgotten how good it feels to walk. How is this possible? I hadn't even noticed that much of a difference, but this . . ." Peter watched as she stopped spinning. She looked down at her feet, and Peter thought it may have been to hide the tears swelling in her eyes. Too late. He'd already seen. "I've missed this."

"Any other sensations besides the return of gravity?"

"Yes. I feel warm and peaceful—calm, like still water." She mused a bit more, scrunching her eyebrows together in concentration. "And the joy is almost spilling over, like a ruptured dam. And I'm so hopeful I expect it will be Christmas when we get back to Hollow Tree Wood."

"That would be something." Seeing her childlike hope brought a smile to his face. "My turn." Peter sprinkled the remainder of the dust over his hair, closing his eyes and waiting for the effects to kick in.

"Do you feel anything yet?"

"Yes," Peter said. "I feel the warmth of sunshine and the calm of slow-moving, white, puffy clouds. I feel the joy of walking along the streets of London a free man, without a care at all. I feel the hope of . . ." He dared not say it out loud. He hoped for Jane. To have her at his side whether in Neverland or in London. "I hope for a miracle."

"Hmm, that last one was vague."

"I feel grounded. Steady. Like I've got my legs back and I can tackle anything."

"That's powerful stuff," Jane said. "You should market it."

"It's not easy to capture. Besides, I don't want anyone knowing about it. Just you. I think this concoction is what made me start longing for the Mother Land again."

"How did you discover it?"

"Like any other scientist—accidentally."

Jane smiled at him. "I'd love to hear the story someday." She sniffed back tears.

"Are you all right, Jane?"

She nodded. "Just a little homesick, that's all. Not that I have a home to go to anymore, but you know."

"Yeah. I do."

"How long will this gravity thing last?"

"Not long. Want to race back to camp?"

"As long as you give me a head start."

Before Peter finished hearing her words, she'd taken off—staggering at first, but she kept trying. Peter chuckled to himself, watching the awkward way she would stumble every few steps and then burst into laughter until she got the hang of it. He'd let her win. Just this once. An eternity of extracting fairy dust and racing with land legs awaited them. Peter would stay. The dust had worked its magic, giving Peter just enough clarity of thought to decide. If he had Jane, staying in Neverland would be a possibility *and* a delight.

THE FALLING PLACE

"A gift? For me?" Jane asked Charlie as he held out a present for her. She unwrapped it and beamed. "Look, Peter. It is Christmas, just like I thought it would be."

"And I've made you something as well," Bryson said. He set a plate of burgers on the table. "The Tally Man brought us one of the pirates' cows."

"Thanks," Jane said. "I think."

"You don't like burgers?" Peter asked, leaning close to her.

"I love burgers," she said, turning to face him.

Peter loved being so close to her, even with everyone watching.

"I just didn't need to know the cow was slaughtered so recently, and probably close by."

"Don't worry Jane. Karl killed it," Simon announced.

"Boys are so disgusting," Misty said.

"No they're not," Frank said. "I am quite refined."

Misty rolled her eyes.

"Here, Peter," Bryson said, slipping Peter a note. "The Tally Man left this for you."

"What is it?"

"Don't know. He said not to read it. Confidential or something like that."

Peter's stomach twisted into a nervous knot. The Tally Man had never corresponded in writing before. Somehow Peter knew the letter couldn't be good.

He shoved it in his pocket, not wanting to ruin the moment.

"Peter, Bryson made something delicious for us to eat, just like we hoped," Jane said.

He was still close enough to keep their conversation from the others. "And yet you still haven't kissed me," he said.

"True," she acknowledged. "I guess it only works some of the time."

Clearly, she thought herself amusing. Rather than be tortured, Peter made a vow to himself that he would simply catch her off guard at some point and steal a kiss from her. She'd never expect that from him. In fact, she'd be more likely to do it. Realizing this, he thought he'd better do it soon before she beat him to it. Perhaps he'd even do it right now in front of everyone.

"Hmmm?" Peter asked when he realized someone had been talking to him.

"Peter's in La-La-Land," said Misty, giggling to herself.

"What did the Tally Man say?" Bryson repeated.

"Oh, nothing to worry about, I'm sure. I'll read it later. Let's eat."

Peter had never been a fan of red meat, but Jane appeared to be enjoying her burger. Her lips shone with grease, and she gladly took another when Bryson offered second helpings. Even Karl joined them for this meal, and for a split second, Peter couldn't believe he'd ever thought of leaving. He also watched the new boy. No more than five or six, the boy would be the perfect playmate for Charlie. The boy appeared to be enjoying his burger, so Peter braved a question.

"And what's your name?"

Peter waited for a response. The boy looked around at everyone before turning to Peter, as if hoping someone would give him a prompt.

"It's okay," Bryson said.

"Yeah, tell him your name." Timothy added.

"His name is Jeremy," Charlie said. "He doesn't talk much yet."

"Yeah, unlike you," Frank said, elbowing the small child.

"Shut up, Frank. At least I don't dress like a weirdo."

This turned into a shoving match. The new boy looked frightened, and Peter cursed the fairy queen, who was probably growing irritable and affecting the mood in the atmosphere.

"That's enough," Peter said.

But the boys would not stop their argument. Peter rolled his eyes, too tired to intervene any further.

Jane stood up. "Misty, would you like to go for a walk? Leave these boys to fight it out?"

"Sure!" Misty swung her legs out from under the table, and they were off, leaving Peter with a hollow feeling.

"At least take the fighting somewhere else," Peter said. "We don't want to watch."

"Fine," Frank said.

"Fine," Charlie mimicked, folding his arms over his chest for good measure.

"Catch me if you can," Frank said before he punched Charlie in the arm and took off running.

"Hey, that's not fair," Charlie complained, but joined in the game of cruelty all the same.

Peter would get to know the new boy in time. No need to rush. Curiosity over the Tally Man's letter nagged at Peter. He excused himself and went to his hollow tree to read the note in private.

Dear Peter,

I hope this find you happy as a Never snapping clam. I want to warn you. I recognize the girl for reason. She is missing person from Hollywood parents. Her picture is all over America and Europe news. If pirates find out, she will be in danger. Her parents offer great reward. I think of taking her myself. She could come back after I get money. I will try not to tell pirates.

TM

Peter couldn't believe the Tally Man would consider taking Jane. Peter fumed, taking larger breaths and fighting the urge to rip the letter to shreds. He kicked a nearby chair instead, and it toppled over and scraped across the floor. He needed to tell Jane—for her sake—but she'd leave for sure. He sat on a chair and crumpled the letter, placing a hand to his forehead and tapping a heel on the floor. Maybe she'd go back to her parents if she knew they were looking for her. Either way, she was in danger. Not only from the pirates but possibly the Tally Man as well. He was usually harmless, but Peter knew he associated with the worst riffraff in Bangkok and London and who knew where else. But he'd warned them. Perhaps he wouldn't do anything.

As Peter mulled it over, he remembered that Jane and Misty had gone off. Alone. The forgetfulness of Neverland was beginning to have stronger effect. Grasping the wadded letter, and still able to feel fully the ground beneath him, Peter ran out his door and into the woods. "Jane!" he called, growing more frantic with each step. "Jane! Misty!"

Peter ran back toward fairy hill, thinking perhaps Jane had taken Misty there, but he couldn't see them. As the fairy dust wore off, his steps lightened, and he could move around with greater ease.

"Jane!" Peter called, surprised by the desperation in his own voice.

"What's the matter, Peter?" Jane asked.

Relief flooded Peter at hearing her concerned voice.

"Are you all right?" he asked. "Where's Misty?"

Jane moved toward him and placed a hand to his brow. "Shhhh, calm down. Misty's already back at camp. I sent her back when I heard you calling us. It sounded serious, so I wanted to make sure she was safe. Then I came to find you."

Peter noticed the sudden presence of nausea, followed by a cold sweat and dizziness. He bent to put his head between his knees, bracing his upper body by placing his hands on his thighs.

"What happened? Are you having another panic attack?" Jane crouched down next to him.

"No, I . . ." Before he could prevent it, or even think to turn away, acid gurgled up Peter's esophagus and shot out of his mouth, right onto Jane's feet. (She rarely wore shoes anymore.)

Mortified, Peter covered his mouth. "Jane, I'm so sorry."

Jane watched her feet for a moment, seeming a bit stunned. "Well I guess we're even," she said. "Peter, what's gotten into you?"

"I think I was worried, and all the running didn't help, and the curative wearing off."

Still bent over, Peter glanced at her, expecting a look of disgust, but there were those eyes, warm and caring, concerned rather than appalled.

"Does this have something to do with that letter from the Tally Man?"

No more secrets, Peter reminded himself. He nodded, forcing deep, even breaths. He stayed low, fearing that if he stood, the dizziness would take hold again.

"What did he say?"

"It's in my pocket." Peter barely heard his own raspy voice.

Jane stood and reached into his pants pocket, pulling out the crumpled letter. She turned away from him and read the words.

"Jane, I understand if . . ." Peter tested his steadiness by straightening a few inches at a time. While the nausea persisted a bit, the dizziness subsided. "I understand if you want to go back."

She turned, dropping her hand so the letter slapped against her leg. "Oh, they're just trying to get attention. My parents love to be on the front of the tabloids. And they don't have any money, so I don't think it's very legit anyway."

"But Jane, if . . ." Peter's chest began to tighten, but he resolved to remain in control.

"But what?"

"What if they . . ." He lowered his head and put a hand to his forehead, unable to bare the thoughts invading his mind, thoughts of Jane in danger. "I just don't want anything to happen to you. I'd never forgive myself."

"Hey, nothing's going to happen to me." She approached him warily, possibly because of the fear that he may not be done throwing up yet. "Look at me," she said, placing her hand on his cheek. "I hope Peter gets what he's hoping for."

"You're going to kiss me when I just vomited?"

She huffed. "Not a chance. I hope Peter gets what he's really hoping for." She stared at him for a moment. "I'm going to head back to camp. Wash my feet. Twice."

"I'll walk you back."

"No, I think you need to stay here and take a few more deep breaths."

"But—"

"I'll be fine."

Peter ached when the warmth of her hand left his face, leaving him with the cool breeze and a question on his mind. What did Jane think he "really" hoped for? He suddenly felt exposed, as if Jane knew more about him than he did. He watched her disappear into the forest. He didn't follow her, though, knowing how close they were to camp. Puzzled and still a bit woozy, Peter continued toward fairy hill. He needed a quiet moment alone before facing the Lost Boys again. He wondered how Jane could be so certain that she'd be okay. Thoughts of her being tortured came to his mind. Peter took some more deep breaths and tried to force the images out of his head. He distracted himself with the surrounding scenery.

He sat at the top of the mound, looking out over Hollow Tree Wood and much of Spring Quarter. The grasses grew long—some yellow, some green—the trees swayed in the gentle breeze, casting a spell on their audience. The fairies danced all around him until one landed on his chest. Peter couldn't put a finger on his current emotional state. Somehow, he thought it closer to distress than peace, but the fairy was white, as if not seeking to draw a positive feeling from Peter but to give him one. The fairy flickered gray, then brown, returning slowly to white after each. Intrigued, Peter continued to watch the fairy. It flickered orange, then purple, and again returned to white. Amazed by this, Peter tried to decide what was happening. It seemed more than anything that the fairy worked to extract the negative emotions from Peter. Soon another white fairy landed and began doing the same thing. Then another. And another. And another. Dozens more flickering fairies came until finally they all glowed white simultaneously. Peter took note of his state, and the results seemed magical. The fairies had drawn the poison out of him and left him without any distress at all. Comforted and ready to face it all again, Peter stood. He whispered a thanks to his friends and headed back to camp, eager to record what had happened in his journal. These creatures never ceased to teach him.

Bryson and Charlie greeted Peter when he arrived. Misty played a game with Timothy and Frank, and Jeremy sat at the table, probably waiting to be fed. He'd be eating and sleeping more than anything else for a while.

"Where's Jane?" Peter asked.

"I thought she went to look for you," Bryson said. "She came back to camp for a bit, then left again."

"Did she say why?"

"Not really, I guess. I just assumed she and you were going somewhere. Her backpack looked full. She even had her shoes on. I thought maybe you two were going to spy on pirates. Is something wrong?" Bryson could probably tell this news put Peter on alert. Peter tried to hide his concern, but he knew the blood drained from his face. His palms grew hot, and he had no control over the instantaneous pounding of his heart.

"I'm sure it's fine," Peter said.

"But where would she go?" Bryson asked.

Peter remembered their journey through Neverland, ending at the Falling Place.

"I'll just go and look for her."

"Peter, tell us what is happening," Bryson said.

Peter looked around. All the children were watching them, probably eavesdropping. Peter stepped close to Bryson, trying to act calm so the children didn't get worried. "I'll just go and find her."

Attempting to hide his urgency, Peter ambled out of camp. He reached into his pocket for some fairy dust and dumped it on his head. Rather than risk more sickness, he went the long way, circling Neverland season by season until finally arriving at the cliff where a lone figure stood under the dark, starry sky looking down into the abyss.

"Leaving-on-a-train-Jane?" Peter asked after landing on the rock beside her, breathless and aching. "Isn't this how we first met?"

She stood on the edge, just inches from the falling place. A gust of wind could have sent her back to Earth.

"Did I ever tell you about the stars here?"

"No, Peter." She sounded a bit forlorn, or perhaps impatient to get going.

"Some people come to Neverland for real, like you and me and all the Lost Boys. And some come only in their dreams or imaginations." He looked upward, hoping to pull her eyes away from her current fixation on the gaping hole threatening to divide the two of them.

"They're all up there. The dreams and wishes of those who've imagined this place, at least that's what I like to believe."

"Peter, that's a lovely idea, but . . ."

"There are so many things I still want to show you."

She jerked her head to face him. "Peter, this place isn't for me. I need to go home." Her eyes filled with tears, but he knew Jane. She had enough courage to leave. Even if she had to go alone, even if she didn't really have a home to go to.

Peter now held in his heart two compartments—one for Jane and one for Neverland. He spent the dwindling moments comparing the sizes of the compartments. Did he love Neverland more? Or Jane? Dancing-in-the-rain-Jane. Sweet-as-a-candy-cane-Jane. Without-her-he'll-go-insane-Jane. The answer, clear in his mind, stayed glued to his tongue. Because while he loved her more than anything, he couldn't leave the Lost Boys alone.

"I want more than this, Peter. I want to grow up. I want to get old and wrinkly. I want to have a job and my own family and children that I cherish, who love me no matter my failings. Thank you for bringing me here. I love this place. I always will."

"Please don't go, Jane," Peter begged.

"It is not your age that makes you a man, but your actions. You don't know it, Peter. But you have grown up already. And the longing for Earth will only increase, and soon you'll find yourself wishing that rather than taking care of everyone else, you had simply lived your own life." She took a step forward and fell before his eyes, sailing quietly down until she vanished from sight. Even though Peter had used the falling place before and knew what would happen to her, it terrified him to see her falling like that.

Peter closed his eyes, fisted his hands, and fought against his longing to throw himself after her. He thought of the ever-growing sorrow and danger around him and his ever-dwindling list of allies.

He fell to his knees and cried out, "Jaaaane! Jane!" His voice echoed throughout Neverland, bouncing off the snowy mountains and grassy hillsides, sweeping down into the desert sand, touching the velvet sky, and coming back to haunt his own ears. And he knew that at hearing his cries, every fairy in Neverland would turn the color black. Maybe some would even die because he let her go.

He wanted to cry but was too numb. "Jane. Jane." How could she just leave? After he'd shown her Neverland, taught her how to kill a mermaid, taught her how to fly? He'd even let her see the most vulnerable side of him. She must not love him. Or she must love Earth more. Perhaps her decision had been just as hard. He knew it must have been. It could have been that Jane knew what she wanted and wasn't afraid to go after it.

"Jaaaaaane!" he screamed into the darkness, pounding his fists against the rocky floor. "Jane! I need you! Come back!" A little voice inside his head told him to stop being a fool and go after her.

But the Lost Boys waited. Many of them would feel sorrow at having lost Jane, but not like Peter. Every moment he would think of her: she lived but remained untouchable, inaccessible. She existed but not to him. And she would grow old without him. Probably marry some stupid bloke. Not him. Have children. Without him. Die. Without him. Losing Jane tortured him. Worse than pirate torture. Knowing one thing—that he loved Jane—but being subjected to another—that he could never have her—would torture him forever. And the compartments in his heart separated, so that one beat for Neverland in a steady, dutiful pattern. And one beat for Jane: slow, solemn, gravitating toward a place it could never go again. Half his heart lived on the Mother Land with her. He let it go and walked back to tell the Lost Boys they'd lost their mother.

THE GRAND PALACE

"*Y*ou let her go?" Bryson asked. Charlie cried nearby, and Misty comforted him.

Peter wondered if his facial expression gave him away. Or perhaps they could tell he'd been crying.

"How could you just let her go?" Timothy asked.

"Yeah, I liked Jane," Frank said.

Peter marveled at the idea himself—how he could just let her go. The fact that he'd done it for them and that they questioned him now, left him feeling a bit resentful.

"Where's Jeremy?" Peter asked Bryson.

"Sleeping in Charlie's hollow tree. We haven't fixed him up his own yet."

"And where's Karl?"

"Beats me," Bryson said.

"I'm right here." Peter turned to see Karl entering camp. "Look what I found, Peter."

Peter glanced to the object Karl held in his hand. Despite his joy at seeing it, panic threatened to chase away any positive feelings of reunification.

"Where did you get that?" Peter asked, looking around the edges of the forest to make sure a band of pirates hadn't followed Karl.

"Isn't this what you got from the mermaids? I was spying on the pirate ship and Sven left it on his desk. I thought you might want it back, so I took it."

Peter held out his hand, and Karl released the familiar object into his palm.

"What is it, Peter?"

"It's my age calculator. Karl you shouldn't have taken it. They'll be coming for it."

"I'm sorry, Peter, but you've become a pansy."

"Shut up Karl! Do you have any idea what you've done?" Peter asked.

"I don't care. You used to be willing to fight the pirates. You used to be fun. Remember when—"

"That's enough," Peter said.

Charlie tugged on Peter's shirt, sniffing back tears. "Peter, I want Jane."

Overcome by curiosity, Peter ignored Karl's accusations and Charlie's plea and studied the numbers on the dial, trying to determine how much Earth time remained before he turned eighteen. Hours, not even enough for one day. Crushed by this realization, Peter sat down on the ground.

"What's wrong with Peter?" Misty asked, clearly bewildered by Peter's somberness.

"What does it mean?" Karl asked. "The markings on the dial."

"There's something I need to tell all of you." Peter proceeded to tell the whole story—what the pirates had threatened during his last capture, how he'd brought Jane here to replace him, his longing to go back to Earth, how the Tally Man had given him an age calculator long ago simply because Peter had expressed curiosity at how old he was getting. "Not that it's one hundred percent accurate," Peter added. "The pirates are just stupid. It calculates time while I'm in Earth's atmosphere and then stops when I leave."

"You were going to leave us?" Bryson asked.

Peter couldn't bear to look at him for long. Bryson seemed to shoulder the weight of this information. Karl and Jeremy seemed indifferent, and all the others seemed to be numb with shock. Bryson's eyes alone revealed betrayal.

"I'm sorry, Bryson. I imagine I would have mustered the courage to tell you eventually."

"If you're leaving, Peter, then you have to bring Jane back," Bryson said.

"I can't. She left because she wanted to. I can't force her to stay. Besides, if I leave, the pirates might kill me."

"We wouldn't let them kill you," Charlie said. The brave words sounded comical coming from such a young voice.

"But you want to return to Earth?" Karl asked.

Peter hated to admit it to them again.

"Is that what you really want?" Bryson asked, arms folded across his chest, and his hurt expression singed Peter's heart.

"It *was*," Peter admitted, resigned to the fact that it simply wasn't possible anymore. Peter longed for the comfort and solitude of his own familiar hollow tree. Head bowed, he stood and walked away from them, desperate for isolation.

"Well, if Peter won't go after Jane, I will!"

Peter whipped his head around to see Misty walking away from camp.

"I know where the falling place is," she said.

Nothing frightened Peter more than the thought of Misty on the streets of Bangkok.

"No, Misty. You mustn't leave," Peter commanded.

"I'm not letting her go alone," Simon said.

"Wait for me," Charlie called.

"Why don't we all go?" Karl asked. "And forget the falling place, let's just fly back."

The mere discussion of this possibility sent Peter into a frenzy—all of them, traveling back to Earth looking for Jane, who probably wouldn't come back if they begged.

"She didn't even say good-bye," Frank said.

"Yeah, let us at least say good-bye," Timothy echoed.

These last sincere pleas nearly broke Peter's heart. She hadn't said good-bye, not to anyone. She wouldn't have said good-bye to him if he hadn't found her at the falling place. Peter realized that because of this, whether she chose to come back or not, Jane had some explaining to do. But he didn't know how to find her. He had no way of calculating how long she had already been gone. Would she go back to London? Search for her parents in the US? All of this swirled in Peter's head until he finally made the decision that he had to go after her. If nothing else, he wanted to know how she could leave without saying good-bye to these children who thought of her as their mother, even if she never saw it that way. Peter also realized that he hadn't told her how he felt about her, how much she meant to him. He could at least do that. It might not make any difference to her, but he had to try.

"Fine, I'll go after her."

"Really?" Bryson asked, his tone of disbelief insulting Peter a bit.

"Yes. Now. I'll try the falling place in case she's still in Bangkok. That will be faster than flying anyway."

"Can I come, Peter?" Charlie asked.

"No, I have to go alone."

"What about the pirates?" Karl asked.

This one risk remained, and Peter knew he'd never forgive himself if any harm came to them. "Here," Peter said, holding his age calculator out to Karl. "Return this to the pirate ship. Hopefully Sven hasn't noticed yet." Peter knelt in front of Charlie. "Will you look after everyone while I'm gone?"

"Okay, except for Misty. She's a girl!"

"Yes, I know. Simon can look after her." Peter smiled at them all. Charlie looked pleased, and Misty rolled her eyes.

Peter turned to Bryson and Karl. "You'll need to be careful. If Sven realizes the dial's gone, he'll most likely attack. Bryson, don't let the others out of your sight. Karl, come straight back after you've returned the dial." Looking at them, Peter remembered that he wasn't alone, that he hadn't been all along. The older Lost Boys always pulled their weight. "Thanks for finding my age calculator, Karl. I'm sorry I yelled at you."

Karl nodded, and Peter reached into his pocket for a pinch of dust. He dropped it on his head and lifted off. Feeling much better physically than he had the last time, he took the shortcut to the falling place, too determined to notice any dizziness that might ensue. As he crossed into Winter Quarter, he looked back to see all of them waving at him. The vertigo set in after that, probably amplified by his head movement. Everything seemed to spin. He landed on the rock that jutted out over the great expanse of nothing, took a deep breath, and jumped.

Free-falling, Peter tried to twist so that his backside faced down. He loved flying head first but falling had a much different feeling. Finally succeeding, Peter watched the starry sky until the stars all but disappeared. Knowing arrival came quickly, Peter braced himself. He pulled his knees in as much as he could and placed his hands underneath them. He tucked his chin in and closed his eyes.

The wormhole sucked him in. Forced to let go of his legs, Peter spun out of control through the tube, his eyes straining from the constant streams of bright light surrounding him. The wormhole slurped and sucked, keeping him in constant, steady motion. He stopped spinning and moved with greater ease, lying on one side with his arms stretched overhead, hands grasping for anything tangible as if to slow things down, but to no avail.

Finally, the wormhole shot Peter out over the Gulf of Thailand and disappeared. The sucking stopped, replaced by the distant chimes of city life. Peter flew across the sky, the fairy dust of no use to him after travelling at such velocity. He gradually slowed and began falling toward the water. Willing himself into flight, Peter swooped up just before landing with a splash. He flew up the Bay of Bangkok and along the Chao Phraya River, where ferries and water taxis carried tourists lazily along. Seeing all the people walking the streets of Bangkok alarmed Peter. How was he ever going to find Jane in a crowd like this? If she was even still in Thailand. Peter began to think of Jane and all the things that he knew about her. He imagined her walking along the winding river and into the city. But where would she go? Did she have any money? How would she get food once the hunger set in again? Would she try to find help?

The image of Jane splashing in a puddle with little Charlie came to Peter's mind, springing an idea. Jane would be touring—seeing the sights and smells of Bangkok, not trying to find her way back to London or the United States. But where to start looking? There seemed only one logical answer. It came into sight, giving him a sense of déjà vu. The Grand Palace. Peter sought out an unpopulated area and landed, observing the palace's pale façade and ornate golden spires. People walked about, their faces shaded from the piercing sun of Bangkok's hot season.

Someone caught Peter's eye, and there, walking smack in front of the palace, wearing the same outfit she'd worn the night she came to Neverland, was Jane.

Peter opened his mouth to call her name, but found his tongue parched. How long since he'd had a drink of water? Now the effects of Earth began to wear on him. His stomach growled with hunger. Worst of all, a raspy voice sounded behind him.

"Hello, Peter. Thought you could slip away unnoticed. Too bad the mermaid passage is faster than the falling place."

After turning around, Peter viewed a familiar face, and his blood ran chill. Russa smiled much as Peter imagined a psychotic killer smiled before attacking his victims, showing off two silver teeth that stood out among their average neighbors.

Peter knew if he called out to Jane she would be in danger as well. He couldn't let them know he'd come after her. No, Peter had sealed his fate. By coming after her, he'd ensured that he would never see her again. Peter swallowed, resisting the temptation to turn and have one last glimpse of her.

"What now, Russa? Or should I say Cole?"

"It doesn't make a difference what you call me, Peter. It won't change your fate."

The pirate's cold tone unnerved Peter. He worried if Karl had also been caught with the age calculator.

Peter felt the point of Russa's blade against his back, only his thin shirt separating it from his skin and all the vulnerability that lay beneath, like arteries that could bleed him to death.

"Just a reminder not to try anything stupid," he spat in Peter's ear before placing the blade back wherever he'd gotten it from. "Sven's waiting for us." Russa kept a hand on Peter's shoulder, guiding him along the sidewalk away from Jane and the Grand Palace.

Peter looked back, hoping for one more glimpse of the girl he'd placed all his hopes on. All Peter found was a sea of unfamiliar tourist faces, each person dressed in suitable clothes for entering the sacred shrine.

Peter recalled his first encounter with the Grand Palace, and how he'd had no idea about the dress code. Sent away at first, Peter had to trade with the Tally Man for some socks and shoes. He glanced at his feet, still grateful the event had cured him of his determination to either go barefoot or wear sandals. If the pirates took him to Black Cavern or the pirate ship, he'd be grateful once again for the shoes on his feet.

"Watch where you're going," Russa barked.

Peter faced forward, obeying Russa's command and barely missing an oncoming barrage of tourists who'd just gotten off a bus.

"Where are you taking me?" Peter asked, nearly choking on the dryness in his throat. He needed water, and soon.

"Oh, I don't know. This place seems good enough to start you on your road to becoming a pirate."

He wondered what Russa meant, what he would have him do. Peter's heart began racing as Russa pushed him toward a group of tourists standing and waiting for a bus.

"I can see that man's wallet bulging through his back pocket."

Peter followed Russa's gaze to see where the smelly pirate looked. His eyes focused on an aged Asian man with white hair. He shielded himself and a woman—most likely his wife—with an umbrella.

"Do it," Russa spat, probably sensing Peter's hesitation. "And don't get caught." Russa reached for his knife again, pulling it slightly from behind his belt. His grin shot a quick chill through Peter's spine.

Peter gulped. Was this really it? His life as a Lost Boy was over? Jane had left him. His mind became a busy intersection of contradictive ideas. He resisted Russa's commands with vigor but also couldn't deny being curious as to what it would feel like to steal the wallet. A cloud of despair threatened to overtake him, while at the same time adrenaline coursed through him, as if he could taste the thrill of the pirate life already. Did any of it even matter anymore, now that she was gone? And how had he allowed himself to get so distracted from his plan? How was it that she had been able to escape Neverland, but not him? Anger seeped into his heart, and he felt it like a thousand miniature tentacles pricking and grasping, threatening to take hold of him completely.

Russa's blade poked into his back, and Peter bit his lip to keep from yelling. His rage deepened, and with a silent, cynical "happy birthday" wish to himself, Peter moved forward with confidence, slipped his hand into the man's back pocket and retrieved the wallet, afterward shoving it into his own pants.

"Oh, excuse me," Peter said when the man looked back at him. Peter pretended that he had only run into the man rather than rob him. Peter tried to smile at the victims, tried to convey that he meant them no malice, but suspected his attempt came across more as a grimace. The man nodded and mumbled an acceptance of Peter's apology in a language Peter didn't quite recognize.

Russa's knife blade poked into his back again. "Move," he grumbled.

They walked on, Russa's knife reminding Peter to keep moving at an acceptable pace. They crossed a street, and Russa put his knife away again. After a mile or so of winding closer to the heart of the city, Russa pulled Peter down an alley where they went through a door.

A confounding darkness and the aroma of whiskey assaulted Peter as the door closed behind them. Russa pulled on Peter's arm, taking the lead this time. They walked down a hallway toward a dim light. Peter knew better than to let the light give him any hope. When it came to pirates, the light never lasted.

As they walked, a soft murmur of voices became audible. Sven's foul voice rose above them all, and Peter pulled back from Russa, his survival instincts kicking in. He knew he needed to get out of there. Russa's grip tightened, and Peter knew the man's fat fingers would leave a bruise on his arm. At last, Russa shoved him through a doorway laden with strings of beads. Peter managed to stay standing, only to fall to the ground when Sven's fist greeted his jaw with a vengeance.

"Welcome to piracy," Sven said. An eruption of nervous laughter came from several pirates surrounding him. Peter recognized Larry and Harry. A wad of spit whipped Peter's face—Sven's first gift after the blow. Looking around once more, Peter saw a few more familiar faces, including the Tally Man. Peter knew better than to feel betrayed, but he envisioned a fairy the metallic color of silver anyway. Sven raised his fist again and brought it crashing down on Peter.

"And don't worry, Peter. That wild Lost Boy will probably wake up. Happy birthday."

Peter closed his eyes, and before passing out, felt the sharp kick of a pirate's boot to his left kidney.

PETER PAN, THE PIRATE

*P*eter had two choices. Chained to a wall in Black Cavern, he tried to reason through his predicament. Two choices were all he could handle: he could either fight—and feel more pain—or he could let them turn him into a pirate. Stealing the wallet had been easy compared to the other things they'd tried to get Peter to do, like rob a bank and kidnap a child for starters. Peter had refused. His head throbbed constantly. His arms burned under the weight of the cuffs holding him chained. Even in the dim light, he could see the bruises and blood dirtying his skin. And he craved food and water constantly. Not that he really needed it now that he was back in Neverland. Craving was different from real hunger and thirst. Constantly in need of something, Peter felt empty, as if he was just out of reach of any sort of relief. Yet the need was insistent. Somehow this proved more torturous than the physical abuse.

Having only two choices didn't really simplify things. Not when both choices were impossible. Part of him wanted to fall asleep and never wake up.

Quick, sure footsteps descended the stairs and approached Peter.

"What will it be, Peter?" Sven asked.

Peter looked to Sven, whose face barely showed itself—a circle of paleness surrounded by the dark of the cavern.

Perhaps with some nourishment, Peter could think of a plan. "If I could only get a bit of something to eat, Sven, or drink?"

A distant thought threatened to shame Peter: something about begging or stooping too low. Peter couldn't quite catch it, and he chased after it for a bit, trying to know his own thoughts again, but it could not be retrieved. Two choices. That was currently the extent of Peter's mind.

"Peter, you can't fool me. I know you can't really be hungry." Sven's boot lifted and rushed into Peter's mouth. He tasted the familiarity of his own blood mixed with the dirt on the bottom of Sven's shoe.

Sven began pacing. "I have to admit I'm losing patience, Peter."

"Then why not just kill me?"

"I am killing you, stupid. Is it not going fast enough for you? I never have been very merciful. You know that. I really don't care if you die, Peter. However, I must admit it would be much more of a conquest if you joined my crew. You have to admit that turning Peter Pan into a pirate would be the ultimate achievement for the Captain of Neverland."

Two choices. Peter pulled on the chains, perhaps his last remaining effort to put up a fight or try to escape. The shackles moved only inches before pulling him back with the sharp pain of renewed cutting on his arms.

"Don't be a fool, Peter. Life as a pirate isn't all bad. We'll start off slowly. You can swab the deck and serve our food. You can merely watch our more dastardly acts for a time." He turned to Peter. "This will desensitize you, see? Eventually it won't be bad anymore. It'll be . . . well, normal."

"It could never be normal to me. I've been alive too long." As soon as he uttered the words Peter knew Sven hadn't heard. Peter barely recognized the sound of his own voice.

"What was that? You'll have to learn not to mumble, Peter, if you want to be understood."

It didn't matter. Two choices. Did he have to decide now? No, he didn't. He could either decide now or decide later. He'd remain quiet.

"What will it be, Peter?"

Peter didn't answer.

"What will it be, Peter? You've got three seconds to answer. Three, two, one."

Sven's boot met Peter's mouth again, this time from the opposite side.

"Bring in the brand!" Peter got a whiff of fish and garlic as Sven yelled this inches from his face. "If that circle on your shoulder hasn't convinced you you're a pirate, perhaps we'll have to put one right over your heart."

Peter fought the panic welling up inside. "No," Peter muttered. "Please." Fists and boots paled in comparison to the end of a hot branding iron. Peter heard the sizzling loud and clear, as if his sense of hearing had just grown keener.

"What's that?" Sven asked. "Is Peter Pan begging?"

"Please." But Peter could barely move his mouth anymore, and this last plea never made it past his lips.

"Oh, do beg," Sven egged. "Begging always makes it more satisfying when I don't give in."

Peter began to see stars. Or were they tiny bumblebees? They swarmed around his head. He didn't know if he was hallucinating or not. Peter tried to wave the objects away only to be stopped by the forceful grasp of a hand on his arm. He resisted, trying to hug his knees to his chest to protect himself from the inevitable. Against his own will, Peter let out a cry.

"Oh, I can't bear it," Sven said. "Will someone please shut him up?"

A large hand grabbed hold of Peter's shirt and yanked him out of his shielded position. Peter wondered if it was Russa but couldn't bear to look. He knew if he opened his eyes, the fear would only increase. His head buzzed, and his whole body heated up, as if preparing for him to pass out. Nausea reared its ugly head, and vomit threatened to surface. Peter clenched his teeth, vowing to remain in control of both his emotions and physical sensations. Lying on his back now, Peter felt someone pull at his shirt until it ripped. He only had time to cringe before the burning began. Peter clenched his fists, and forced himself to remain quiet and still.

The iron was removed, and a large amount of cold water fell on Peter. He sputtered to prevent from choking.

"Say it, Peter. Say, 'I'm a pirate,'" Sven said. "That's all you have to do."

Peter kept his lips sealed until the iron was pressed to his skin again. He shoved down a yell while considering whether to give in or not.

"Say it," Sven said, and in response the man holding the iron shoved it into Peter's chest even harder.

Peter wriggled against the floor, digging his heels into the ground. He kept his eyes shut tight and imagined a pool of cool water. He dreamed of jumping in the stream near the pirate's farm or Brim Lake, even if it meant facing the fearsome mermaids. A vague memory came to him, a memory of tossing someone in that stream, but once again, the memory slipped away. The glimpse of something else outside the darkness of Black Cavern calmed his mind enough to prevent a scream. Two choices. This or be a pirate. "I'm a pirate," Peter muttered, though the sudden utterance surprised even him.

Sven stopped his shuffling. "What was that?"

Through an aching groan, Peter said it again. "I'm a pirate. I'll do whatever you ask. Just please stop."

After one final shove, the iron was finally lifted. Unable to move, Peter remained sprawled on the stony floor. Another splash of freezing water fell on him, and Peter began to shiver.

"And how are you going to prove it? How do I know you won't go back on your word?" Sven asked.

A stone seemed to be forming in Peter's heart. A cold one. Peter forced the tears back. "I will never go back on my word. Not this time. I will be a pirate until I die." In truth, Peter hoped the dying part came sooner rather than later.

Sven crouched close to Peter's ear, his stench making Peter gag. "If you so much as blink wrong, I'll kill you." Standing up, Sven brushed his hands together, creating a sound that irritated Peter. "Well, I think this calls for a celebration, don't you, Russa?"

Peter finally opened his eyes, catching a faint glimpse of Russa's expression. Perhaps Russa wanted to see Peter dead. Or perhaps a bit of goodness remained, and he didn't like to see Peter this way. At any rate, a bit of relief set in as Peter realized he could feel and think a little more clearly again.

"Don't you think a celebration is in order, Peter?"

"Will it involve cold water?" Peter asked.

Sven let out a deep laugh. "He's gaining his sense of humor back already."

Russa laughed along, but Peter thought the laugh sounded forced.

"Come, Russa. Let's tell the others and make plans. We'll travel to Bangkok to bring back whiskey and bourbon. We'll think of the perfect initiation for Peter and get any needed supplies from the Tally Man."

Peter could sense they were about to leave. "Wait," he called. "Aren't you going to let me go?"

"Not until we get back. You can't walk through Bangkok looking like that. Try not to bruise or scar yourself any further, Peter. We pirates like to keep our faces pretty." While Peter didn't see, he knew Sven smiled at his own faulty comment.

"Who's going to stay and guard him?" Russa asked.

"Whoever I find the most disagreeable when we get back to the ship," answered Sven.

Their voices began to blur when a ringing flooded Peter's ear. It seemed a flame rose from Peter's chest, and while he wished to escape it, he knew it belonged to him now—the burning, the cold stone in his heart, the brand on his chest and the futureless, degrading life of a pirate. Peter pondered for a moment what he would come to smell like. All the pirates had a distinct scent, some of garlic, some of horrible breath.

Peter realized they'd gone. The ringing in his ear began to soften, and Peter felt a potential blackout coming on. He stared up into the darkness, too weak to move. A tiny light flickered into the cavern and came toward him. Peter squinted until he perceived the light belonged to a fairy. Its lavender hue pricked a memory for Peter. He knew the color should be significant somehow, but as with everything else, the exact meaning seemed just out of reach.

A soft, echoing voice descended on Peter. He watched the fairy flit away and focused on the voice, trying to determine if it belonged to one of his torturers. But the speaker couldn't be a pirate. The words held a different quality, less gruff and more . . . female. Peter closed his eyes and just listened, trying to understand the words being uttered.

Finally, something clicked when the voice called Peter's name. Peter opened his eyes and saw a white light at the cave entrance. Its brightness forced his eyes closed again, and his head buzzed. In that moment, he understood. Peter didn't have to become a pirate. This was the end. Peter was dying, and an angel had come to take him away.

RESCUE

*P*eter dreamed a bird flew over his head. Standing on his feet, he looked up and watched it swoop toward him as he swayed this way and that. But it wasn't a bird at all. A girl floated just out of reach, wearing a cream-colored old-fashioned nightgown, the same kind Wendy had worn the night they first met.

"Peter," she called softly as she landed before him.

"Wendy," Peter replied. "Is that really you?"

"Peter."

Wendy placed her hand on Peter's shoulder and shook him. A sharp pain erupted from his side and a familiar searing came from the disturbance of her shaking.

"Peter," she persisted.

The dream left him, even when he searched after it and tried to bring it back. Becoming more and more aware of each ache and pain, Peter muttered and groaned, still lying on the ground.

"Peter? Are you awake?"

Peter moved his head from side to side, wondering why the voice remained if the dream had gone. He opened his eyes to see a face before him. A girl—not in a white nightgown, but in a graphic tee, pleated skirt, and boots. She held a flashlight that illuminated their immediate surroundings. The sight of his chains cast a weight of sorrow over him.

"Remember me?" the girl asked.

He knew it wasn't Wendy. "You look familiar." Peter began to move, and she reached out to help lift him to a sitting position. His bruised kidneys and cracked ribs begged for relief, but he knew there would be none. Even the slight pressing and pulling of her hands on his arms caused him pain.

"I brought you something," she said. With the flashlight in one hand, she reached into one of her boots and retrieved a small pouch. Whatever it was, Peter doubted it would help. She loosened the pouch and let Peter peer inside.

"Fairy dust," he whispered. "Where did you get that?"

"I stole it from your hollow tree."

Peter began to remember at the sound of her voice, the tone of her answer—matter-of-fact attitude with a bit of . . . facetiousness. A girl he'd brought with him. He got a glimpse of her dancing in the rain and recalled that she was the one he'd thrown in the creek.

"Jane," he said. "It's you." The features of her face seemed to change before him, familiarity coming back all in a single rush.

"I've come to rescue you, Peter."

"You've come to rescue me?" Peter's voice sounded scratchy and weak, and as he spoke, he remembered he'd lost a tooth after one of Sven's kicks to the face. His tongue felt the space where it used to be.

"I saw you get taken by that creepy pirate . . . when I was standing outside the Grand Palace in Bangkok. Don't you remember? I could have sworn we made eye contact."

Peter searched his memories, and they seemed to be coming back bit by bit. "Yes, I remember seeing you, but I didn't think you had seen me."

"Why did you come after me, Peter?"

Peter's head began to throb. He'd been trying too hard to remember, doing too much thinking. An overwhelming exhaustion threatened to grant him unconsciousness again.

But the memories came. He thought of Charlie and the Lost Boys, their disappointment that Jane had gone, and the reason he'd brought Jane to Neverland in the first place. The memories brought on a renewed homesickness for the Mother Land. Lastly, Peter remembered how he'd come to feel about Jane. The cold stone in his heart began to melt as he looked into her eyes. She waited for a response, but Peter grew nervous. He couldn't express how he'd grown to love her—not now. He wasn't prepared. He glanced at her lips, though. More than anything else, he thought a kiss from Jane would improve his current condition.

Peter heard voices outside the cavern.

"Jane, you have to hide. They're coming."

"Where? There's nowhere to hide in here."

"Just turn the light off and crouch in a corner until they're gone again."

The light vanished. Peter heard her shuffles but couldn't quite guess where she'd gone. The tapping of footsteps echoed in the darkness.

"Turn the lantern on, I can't see."

Jack Raven lit a lantern, his cheesy grin on display. Larry stood at his side, not looking happy that he'd been chosen to stay behind and babysit the newest Neverland pirate.

Peter could see Jane in the far corner behind them, squatting with her arms wrapped around her legs and her head bowed. Knowing they'd see her if they turned in the right direction, he tried not to look her way.

"Welcome to the crew," Jack said. Peter couldn't help smiling, no matter how evil the man standing before him. Jack's smile was like a contagion that Peter didn't want to catch but couldn't help catching just the same. Peter cringed when the mere act of smiling caused a sear of pain.

"What shall we have him do first?" Jack asked, turning to Larry.

"Swab the deck," Larry growled. "I'm tired of doing it."

"Are you going to let me go?" Peter hoped more than anything else to get out of the thick cuffs around his wrists.

Jack tilted his head back in laughter. "Not until Sven gets back."

Jane shuffled a bit, distracting Peter from the pirates. He had to remind himself not to look at her, but he could tell she fidgeted with her backpack. She retrieved something from one of the pockets.

"I could swab the deck," Peter said, trying to pull his attention away from her. His voice sounded stronger than before, but only just.

Jack stopped smiling. "I told you. Not until Sven gets back." For as happy as he looked when he was smiling, Jack looked equally evil when he wanted to. Peter didn't know what they planned to do to him. He thought the abuse would stop when he agreed to become a pirate, but perhaps that was just when it really began. Not in the same way he'd been abused so far, but in a more "smack him around, cut him down until he knew his place" kind of way.

From the corner of his eye, Peter noticed Jane stand and face them. She held a pouch in her hand and wore a glove. It took him a moment to realize the significance of it all, but when he did, he had to try with great effort not to panic. He knew he couldn't come to her aid if she failed.

Jane cleared her throat and said, "Hello, boys."

Both pirates spun around and drew swords.

Jane laughed at them, and even though she seemed perfectly confident, Peter could not shove down his concern for her safety.

With her back against the wall, Jane inched toward him.

"Stop moving!" Jack said.

"Yeah, put the pouch down," Larry growled.

"Come and make me," Jane taunted in the sassy way only Jane would dare at such a moment. She shook the bag in their direction.

"Careful," Peter muttered.

Jack lifted his sword and came at Jane.

"No!" Peter yelled.

Everything slowed as Peter watched, still too far away to help at all. Jane dipped and tilted her head to avoid Jack's swing and threw a cloud of black fairy dust at his face. Looking stunned, he dropped his sword. The lantern crashed to the ground as well, the glass breaking and the light teetering but not going out. The smile now galaxies away (and even the ability to appear threatening), Jack fell to his knees and sobbed. "Why me?" he wailed through the tears. His words would have sounded pathetic if it weren't for the sincerity present in his voice.

Larry looked at Jack and then at Jane. His sword still raised, he stood there in a stance of indecision.

"You want some too, loser?" Jane asked. "Come and get it." Peter had the feeling she wanted the pirate to come after her. He could also sense Jane was fighting the effects of the powder herself. She began to look sad— just the beginnings of sadness, like a child who just realized they couldn't see their mother in a crowd of strangers.

Jack's moans grew even more distressing, and Peter couldn't bear to hear. The sorrow threatened to spread over Peter, black fairy dust or not.

Larry took one more look at Jack, a pout forming on his own face, and turned to leave his comrade to fend off the depression alone. Jack lay down on the ground and began to squirm, as if trying to escape the gloom. His tears fell to the floor in a constant rhythm.

Jane dropped the pouch of black powder along with the glove and rushed to Peter, kneeling at his side. "We have to get you out of here."

"How?" Peter asked. "I don't even know where the key is. Sven's probably got it with him in Bangkok."

Jane ignored him and swung her backpack off her shoulders and plopped it down in front of her. She unzipped the large opening and pulled out a large pair of chain cutters. Peter couldn't believe it. He would have guessed she'd pull out a thousand other things, but not this.

"Where in the Neverland stars did you get those?"

"That's just the thing," she said. "You can't get these in Neverland. I had the Tally Man bring me some."

Peter suppressed a laugh, knowing it would cause him pain. "You bargained with the Tally Man?"

"Yep. Got lots of information from him too. He's the one who told me where I could find you and helped me get back here." She worked while she spoke, and Peter felt the weight of the whole cavern lift after she clipped him free.

"I thought you were an angel," Peter said, remembering how he'd seen her come in with the bright light just before he passed out. "I thought I was dying when you came in. I thought you had come to take me away."

"Well, you're right about one of those. Let's get out of here before crybaby comes to his senses."

For a moment, Peter wondered how she could be so cruel. After putting her backpack on, she placed an arm around Peter and helped him stand. Freedom called to him from outside the cavern, and he hobbled along with Jane at his side, trying his best to ward off the sadness permeating the room.

"Does it hurt to walk?" Jane asked.

"My worst injuries aren't on my legs. I'm mostly just stiff. Help me up the stairs, and I think I can walk on my own then."

"What about flying?" Jane asked.

"Even better. The fairy dust will help with the pain and bring faster healing as well."

As they reached the top of the stairs, Jane let go of Peter and readied a new glove and pouch of black fairy dust. She went in front and made sure Larry had truly gone. Peter closed his eyes, half expecting an ambush.

"He's down at the ship," she said. "I can see him watching me with some binoculars."

Peter opened one eye and caught a glimpse of Jane shaking her head as she put the powder and glove in her backpack.

"What an idiot," she muttered as she still watched Larry. She turned to Peter, who had barely opened his other eye. He couldn't decide which he liked seeing more: Jane or the open sky.

"C'mon," she said. "Coast is clear." She pulled a new pouch from her boot—the one she'd shown him earlier—and reached in for some dust. After sprinkling a generous amount on herself, she held it out to him.

All Peter could do was stare at her. Even more memories came back to him: Jane at the train station, Jane killing the mermaid, and Jane kissing him and holding his hand.

"What?" Jane asked.

"Why did you leave?" Peter asked, vacillating between his fondness for her and his anxiety over what answer she might give.

She shrugged. "Because I hoped you'd come after me. I knew how much you wanted to leave this place, but I could also see how conflicted you were over it. Rather than push you off the falling place, I decided to jump myself."

"But how did you guess I'd follow you? I didn't at first, you know. The Lost Boys had to convince me."

Jane pinched some dust and threw it at Peter. He began to feel the lingering sorrow from the cave lift. It disappeared completely when she reached out her hand to him. Peter just looked at it for a moment, comparing it to his own hand covered in bruises.

"I didn't know. I just remembered how all those hopes we expressed came true. So I hoped again, and jumped."

"I thought maybe you went back to find your parents." Even despite the fairy dust, Peter couldn't contain his emotion. A tear swelled in his eye, threatening to give him away once again. "I thought I'd never see you again."

"C'mon, Peter. No time for crying. Let's go say good-bye to the Lost Boys, and I'll tell you all about it on the way."

This caught Peter by surprise. "Say good-bye?"

"Yes, Peter. We're not going to leave without saying good-bye. Not this time."

Peter took her hand. For all his wishing and hoping, leaving Neverland had never seemed real. Now he knew it was not only possible, but necessary. He'd turned eighteen. Staying meant piracy. Leaving meant freedom if they could escape unnoticed. Jane had pulled him back to Earth for those final seconds. Perhaps she hadn't meant for him to be captured by pirates and tortured ruthlessly, but she had meant for him to follow her, and in doing that, his fate had been sealed. Regret mingled with relief. He knew the Lost Boys would be devastated, but he also knew he'd be getting what he wanted all along: a sure escape. And on top of that, he held her hand in his. Cutting-his-chain-Jane.

It would be dangerous, and they'd have to go into hiding. And Peter had given his word to become a pirate, but he reasoned that promises didn't count when extracted through torture.

"Ready?" she asked.

They lifted off together and flew away from Black Cavern toward Spring Quarter. Jane talked about the time she spent in Bangkok. She'd been there only a couple of days before Peter found her at the Grand Palace. She lived it up as a tourist, courtesy of the large amount of money she'd received from the Tally Man in exchange for the stash of fairy dust she took from Peter's tree before leaving.

"I had no intention of finding my parents when I left Neverland, but maybe when we get back, I'll give them a call to let them know I'm alive at least."

The conversation turned Peter's mind to something he hadn't thought about for ages: his future. What were they going to do when they returned? Would she go back to London? Stay in Bangkok? Travel the world? Go to school? A knot formed in his stomach when he thought that whatever her plans were, they might not include him. And if they didn't, what then?

Jane told Peter how she'd tricked the Tally Man into giving her information, after convincing him her parents would never pay the promised reward money.

"I also threatened to gouge his eyes out if he tried to kidnap me or ratted me out to the pirates. Apparently, he found me authentically threatening."

"I don't have any trouble believing that," Peter said. She seemed so comfortable with him, but he knew Jane. She'd be comfortable anywhere. He tried to summon the bravery to ask her what she planned to do when they left and if she had any feelings for him, but finding the courage was a little like summoning a mermaid to the desert.

"Almost there," Jane said. Peter turned from her to the view before them. They crossed from the snow of Winter Quarter to the meadows of Spring Quarter and began to descend into the Hollow Tree Wood.

Peter grew hot and thought he would even begin to sweat. They landed, and Jane pulled him toward the Lost Boys. Peter resisted, tugging on her hand until she stopped and turned to face him. He had to know where she stood—what she hoped to do when they returned and if any of those plans included him in any way.

"Jane, I . . ." The words he'd been trying to formulate escaped his mind. Her ability to suck the thoughts out of his head infuriated him.

"What is it?"

"I wonder . . ." He glanced at her lips.

Jane let go of his hand and stepped closer. She reached out and carefully brushed her fingers across the brand on his chest. "I'm sorry I didn't get here sooner."

Peter looked down to see the marks under the rip in his shirt. "Looks like it's already starting to scar. How's my face?"

"Not too bad. The Lost Boys will be concerned, but it isn't as frightening as it was when we first came out of the cave. All wounds heal. That's what my nanny used to say."

"Do you plan to find her again? When you get back to Earth?"

Jane nodded.

"What else?"

She shrugged. "Haven't thought that much about it yet, I guess. What about you?"

Peter looked up at the sky and breathed deep. "I don't know. Get a job, go to school."

"And what does Peter Pan want to be when he grows up? Perhaps a salesman or an entrepreneur? I've seen you with the Tally Man."

"I don't think so."

"What then?"

"I think I'd like to be something really ordinary. Like a dentist." He smiled at her to let her know that perhaps he wasn't quite sincere.

"Peter Pan, DDS. Has a nice ring to it."

"I think I'll need a new name."

"Me too. Otherwise my parents might find me and try to take all my cash when I'm rich."

Peter liked the idea of sharing a name with her but thought he was probably reading into her words a bit. "Jane, I . . ."

Peter didn't know what would have come out of his mouth, but it didn't matter. Jane put a finger to his lips to stop him. "Shhhhh," she said, a rare intensity in her usually playful eyes. "Look, Peter. I don't know what is going to happen between us, but I'm not ready to give you up, okay?" She pulled her hand away from his mouth and touched her lips to his. After kissing him, she pulled away and reiterated her question. "Okay?"

Peter looked into her eyes, happy to obey. "Okay." Forever was lost to him. For now, he'd be content to live his life one day at a time.

FAREWELL AND ESCAPE

"*N*ervous?" Jane asked after accepting another kiss.

Peter watched her expression, noting the concern present in her face, though she still managed a smile. "About saying good-bye?"

Jane nodded.

"Terrified."

"Don't worry," she said. "I bet they've hardly even missed us."

Jane took his hand and led him into the clearing where the Lost Boys whittled sticks.

"Peter!" Charlie yelled upon seeing them. He dropped his knife and stick and ran into Peter's arms. Peter attempted to swing him around, but the lingering pain halted the act. Peter settled for tousling the boy's hair instead. A wave of homecoming joy swept over Peter, followed by the thought of how much he'd miss Charlie's open arms, sloppy kisses, and shouts of glee.

"Come see what I'm making," Charlie said. He grabbed Peter's hand and yanked, stomping his feet to where he'd dropped his whittling supplies.

"What is it?" Peter asked, taking in the odd-shaped stick. It had a large knot in the middle and several shoots coming out from the largest branch.

"It's a giraffe," Charlie answered, sounding disappointed that Peter hadn't been able to tell. "See, here are the legs, and there's the head, and this is the belly."

"The knot is the belly?" Peter asked, trying to humor the boy, even though Peter didn't really see a giraffe.

Charlie nodded his head and got back to work on his animal.

The smell of a freshly doused fire filled Peter's nostrils. He'd have to get accustomed to other smells—like indoor cooking for example. Peter watched Jane pick up a stick and knife and begin to whittle. Charlie leaned in close to him.

"Peter, who is she?" he asked.

Peter marveled and studied the little boy's honest expression and question. He didn't remember her.

"That's Jane," Peter answered.

"And is she gonna be our new mother?"

As much as Peter had been avoiding this moment, and as much as part of him wanted to go on avoiding, the only way to get on with it was to get on with it.

"No, Charlie. She's not. She's just visiting and will be returning to the Mother Land soon." Charlie's large eyes watched Peter with great interest, soaking up every word. Peter just hoped he'd understand the rest. "And I'll be going with her."

"Okay," Charlie said. "She seems nice. Too bad she's not staying."

Peter knew he'd need to be direct with Charlie. He clearly wasn't picking up on cues.

"Charlie, when I go with Jane, I won't be coming back."

Charlie looked to the ground, as if it held the further explanations he needed.

"Do you understand?" Peter asked.

"You're ready to go back?" Charlie asked, looking at Peter. "Like Lester and Preston and Jeremy?"

Peter looked to Bryson. "Jeremy's gone?"

"Yeah," Bryson started, as if it wasn't a big deal. "Little bloke didn't last long. Karl took him while I stayed with the others."

Peter remembered Sven's mention of Karl in Bangkok. "Karl's okay?"

"Yeah, why wouldn't he be?" Bryson said.

"See, Peter," Jane said. "They've hardly missed us." She smirked at him then winked at Charlie, who rolled his eyes at her.

"Where's Karl now?" Peter asked, trying to shift from a feeling of responsibility to pure curiosity.

"Trying to find the Tally Man. We're almost out of cookies."

Peter looked around at everyone. Misty watched Jane with interest, and Peter was curious whether she remembered her or was simply fascinated by the presence of another female. Jane had been right again—the Lost Boys truly hadn't missed them much. All this time, Peter thought that if he left, Neverland would crumble, and the Lost Boys would be . . . well, lost without him. His own hesitancy had been preventing him all along, his own fears and unwillingness to take risks and embrace change. Perhaps there lingered a part of him that still did not want to grow up. Though, if so, it must be a very small part. As Peter watched Jane, he caught a glimpse of the future—the future that had always been coming no matter how hard and for how long he tried to avoid it—and he couldn't wait to start moving forward. With her.

"Bryson," Peter called out, following with the names of each of the others. "Timothy, Misty, Simon, Frank, Charlie. There's something I'd like to tell you all. Jane and I are returning to Earth." Most of them looked at him, but Simon continued to whittle. "And we're not coming back." That caught Simon's attention. He didn't look at Peter, but he did stop the harsh scratching of his knife against wood.

"You're leaving, Peter?" Bryson asked.

Peter nodded.

"But you've been here forever," Bryson said.

"I know that better than anyone, friend. Will you look after them?"

"I guess," Bryson said, shrugging.

"And harvest the fairy dust?"

"I'll do that!" Misty shouted.

Peter laughed at her enthusiasm. "You can learn as well. Just don't give any to the pirates. And stay away from the mermaids." Peter winked at the girl. He would miss those curls. He would miss them all.

Jane cleared her throat. "Well, I think we'd better be off. Don't you, Peter?" She rubbed her hands over her thighs before standing up.

"I want to go," Frank said. "If Peter's brave enough to go, then I want to go too."

Peter jerked his head toward the boy, surprised at this announcement. "You do?" Peter asked.

"I'm ready to go too," Timothy said.

"Me too," Simon said.

"But what about the fairy dust?" Misty asked.

"You don't have to go now," Bryson said. "Take some time to think about it. You've got more than you'll ever need here."

Peter hadn't been expecting this chain reaction. "I think that's a good idea," Peter said. "Take some time to think about it. I've done that for a good long while, and I'm ready to go now."

Charlie tugged on Peter's shirt. "Peter," he whispered. "I don't want to go back to Earth. It smells like cheese."

Jane burst out laughing, and Charlie looked a bit sad that someone had heard him.

"It's okay," Peter said, trying to keep a straight face. How he would miss Charlie. "You can go back when you're ready. It takes some of us longer than others."

"Good-bye, Peter," Charlie said. He left Peter and sat down by Bryson. Peter mused that it would be better this way: no hugs, no lengthy speeches, and no ceremony. Just simple good-byes.

"Good-bye, Peter," Timothy said. Simon and Frank echoed the same. Misty rose from her seat and gave both Peter and Jane a hug. Following a quick wave, she began skipping around the camp.

Peter watched them for a split second, noting the way they each coped with the discomfort of parting. He reached out for Jane's hand, grateful for the friend he'd found to help him cope with the pang in his heart.

Bryson stood and hugged Peter as well. "Thank you, Peter. For taking such good care of all of us. Until now, I didn't realize that's what you did, but thank you."

"You're welcome," Peter said, and those would be his last words to the Lost Boys because Jane squeezed his hand and pulled him away from them and into Hollow Tree Wood.

"You okay?" she asked as they reached a meadow of canzars—tulip-like flowers, only much taller and each the color of the clear-blue sky.

"I will be," Peter said. As they began to climb a hill, a deafening moan rang out all around them. Jane plugged her ears, but it didn't alarm Peter because he knew what it was. He pulled her by the elbow to the top of the hill and pointed back to Hollow Tree Wood.

"It's dying," he said. "The sick tree."

Jane took her hands off her ears and listened to the sound of dying. "It sounds like it's in pain."

"It probably is," Peter said. "Keep watching, though. It will be over soon."

With a roar, the tree erupted into flames. Smoke began to rise high into the Never sky, and the moaning trailed off.

"That . . . was . . . amazing," Jane said, smiling as she watched the burning tree. Her hands held on to the straps of her backpack, and Peter couldn't resist the urge to kiss her cheek.

"Are we taking any fairy dust with us?" he asked her after planting his lips on her soft skin.

"I don't know," she said, still watching the tree. "Hadn't really thought about it."

"I guess I'm worried I'll be tempted to come back."

She looked at him. "What would be so bad about that?"

He shrugged. "It needs to be for real. Going back, growing old, letting go."

Jane slid off her backpack and knelt on the ground, unzipping the large pocket. She began taking out pouches of fairy dust, and Peter couldn't believe how much she'd nabbed from his hollow tree. She held the black pouch with care. "We'll leave it here," she said. "All of it. Finders keepers. Perhaps there are other uses just waiting to be discovered."

"I left everything in my hollow tree. All my journals, belongings, everything."

Jane stood and looked him deep in the eyes, placing her hands on his cheeks. "Letting go," she reminded him. "They may need your journals, and I rummaged through the entire tree and didn't find anything else really useful."

"What would I do without you?" he asked, sincerely wondering what he had ever done without her.

"Probably pillage and murder. You did get branded as a pirate, you know." Her hands moved to his chest and ran across his fleshy pink scar, the color of a fairy who was lost. That's exactly how he would be without her. Lost.

"Neverland doesn't have to be the place where you live. It can simply be the place you carry in your heart," she said.

Peter smiled at her. They hiked up the rugged rocks that led into Winter Quarter, both feeling the dizziness that came from moving across Neverland in the wrong direction.

"Look," Jane said when they reached the top. "Looks like the pirates are back."

There, in Endal Ocean, Peter could see Sven's ship sailing away from Black Cavern. Apparently they'd run out of fairy dust and would have to search for Peter the old-fashioned way.

"We may have to lay low for a while, start off in some place other than London or Bangkok."

"Sounds good to me," Jane said. "Although, I didn't see nearly enough of Bangkok last time. I've heard they have good dental schools in Russia, though."

Peter laughed at her comment, then turned away from the pirates and stepped to the edge of the falling place. The memory of the last time he'd stood in this spot came to him: his crying out to Jane. She grabbed hold of his hand, as if to remind him that she wasn't leaving without him this time. He let the pressure of her hand comfort him.

"On three?" she asked.

Peter nodded and closed his eyes.

"Okay, one. Two . . ."

Peter bent his knees in preparation, but Jane stopped counting. He fought the growing need to open at least one eye and see what was taking her so long.

"Hold on," she said. "I think you're going to want to see this."

Peter opened his eyes and saw that several fairies danced in front of him, all of them a glowing royal blue—the color of gratitude.

"Turn around," Jane said, placing her hands on his shoulders and forcing him to turn a half circle. Peter's eyes bulged when he saw the massive cloud of fairies—most of them royal blue—flying up toward them. He couldn't see their end, and he had rarely seen so many at one time.

Jane peered up at his face. "They've come to say good-bye, Peter."

"They never could refuse the chance to show off," he muttered.

Jane moved closer and grasped his hand once more. "Backwards?" she asked.

"Why not?" Peter said.

"This time leave your eyes open. One. Two. Three."

Peter and Jane both took a step backward and fell, the swarm of royal blue changing before their eyes into a rainbow of glowing specks that became smaller and smaller until they disappeared altogether.

EPILOGUE

*P*eter closed the bathroom cabinet and leaned toward the mirror, inspecting his smooth chin. Jane would love it. He smiled as he thought of the way she playfully recoiled every time he tried to kiss her over the last several months. Since facial hair was an anomaly on Neverland, Peter had made experimenting a bit of a hobby over the years—sideburns here, a goatee there, nothing too crazy.

"How many jumps do you have today? And what times are they?" Jane called from the bedroom. "I want to know when I need to worry about you free-falling from the sky."

"Three," he called back. "Nine, ten-thirty, and twelve." Jane had never been thrilled about his chosen profession of being a skydiving instructor, but she never would have denied him either.

Peter inspected the crow's feet taking shape around the corners of his eyes until a sparkle caught his attention. A white, wiry hair stuck out from the side of his head, just above his right ear. He reached for it, using the mirror as a guide until he grasped it between his fingers. He debated yanking it, but only for a second. The word *monumental* came to mind. Peter knew what this meant.

His mind drifted back to all those years ago. After leaving Neverland, he and Jane had struggled for months just to scrape for food. She sang on street corners for every meal and for their train tickets back to London where they were able to find Jane's nanny. Too afraid to seek out the Tally Man, they knew it best to disappear as soon as possible. Jane's nanny, Olivia, was ecstatic to see her. They embraced for so long that Peter grew uncomfortable waiting on the front porch of where Olivia worked as a nanny for a wealthy family. Then one of the children came to the door.

Peter grew faint as he remembered. He leaned on the bathroom sink and drew in a deep breath. Even the short interaction with the child had sent him into a panic.

Jane had never left his side. Through name changes, fake IDs, therapy, and dead-end jobs, she'd been more loyal than the Never blue sky in Summer Quarter. After she asked him if he was ever going to propose, they married, but with one stipulation.

"No children?" Jane asked, looking so forlorn it nearly broke Peter's heart. "Ever? What about therapy? You haven't had a panic attack in months, not even around children."

"You almost done in there?" Jane called, snapping Peter out of the past. He turned on the faucet to finish rinsing his razor, his eyes glancing at the edges of the scars on his chest and shoulder, where the pirates had branded him. Some things never seemed to fade with time.

Jane opened the door. "I've got to go. I'll see you at the pub later? I'll be singing something new that I wrote last week."

"Of course. Wouldn't miss it."

"Sounds serious," she said, giving him a pouty look. "Want to tell me about it?"

Peter sighed. She really did need to get going, but he didn't think he could wait the entire day to tell her. "Do you remember when I proposed?"

"You mean when *I* proposed?" She pointed to her chest, her collection of bracelets sliding down her arm. She wore skinny jeans, ankle boots, and a graphic tee that said "Have a mice day" and was complete with a picture of a small, realistic-looking mouse. She'd begun designing graphic T-shirts shortly after Peter finished training as a sky-diving instructor. Many of her T-shirts were designed with a bit of Neverland inspiration, like the one with a drawing of the Tally Man's face on a coffee mug that said, "Have you seen this mug?"

Peter forced a grin. "No, I proposed."

"After I gave you the idea."

Peter shook his head, opting to give up the age-old argument rather than engage in her invitation to banter.

"Look," he said, pointing to his head.

"Look at what?" She stepped into the bathroom and peered up above his right ear.

"Do you see it?"

"See what?" Then she gasped and covered her mouth, probably hiding an enormous smile. "Peter, you've got a gray hair."

Peter looked in the mirror once more. "I think it's white actually."

"Peaceful," she said. "Aging is peaceful, just like the white fairies, remember?"

Peter nodded. "I remember." He leaned on the sink again, awash with emotion. He peered at his reflection once more, thinking of what he would look like when all his light brown became "peaceful."

"Are you okay?"

"You don't remember what I said when I proposed, do you?" He glanced in her direction, his hands still pressed against the counter for support.

"That's because I proposed to you." She tilted her head and grinned, taunting him with those facetious eyes. "You shaved?" She reached out and rubbed his face. "Finally," she said, and Peter received her peck to the side of his mouth with glee.

He grabbed her hand and held it to his face before she could take it back. "I'm sorry I didn't propose first," he said. "But do you remember what I told you? And what I said about getting older and gray hair?"

Her cell phone began to ring, and she fumbled, trying to grab it with her free hand, until Peter took it and silenced it. Only then did it seem to dawn on her. Her expression sobered, and all her previous rushing seemed to vanish. "Peter, if this is a joke—"

"I'm not joking. You know that really isn't my style, especially when it could hurt you."

"You told me you wouldn't consider having children until you started to get gray hairs." She looked as though she was trying to process not only the memory, but the idea of it. Jane's brain was probably filling with imaginings of their own little brood.

Peter nodded. The idea had been his compromise. After the experience with the child Jane's nanny watched, Peter was afraid he wouldn't be able to handle children of his own. But this idea devastated Jane. So he came up with the idea of waiting until he started to go gray.

Her eyes brightened. "Children?"

Peter smiled at her. How could he not when she grinned like that? "Our own children?"

"Well, I was thinking we could start with one. See how it goes."

Jane let out a laugh and threw her arms around his neck, nearly knocking him over. Her legs dangled, bent at the knee, and Peter held fast, sinking his face into her neck. She sniffed, and he pulled away to check for tears, which she not only wiped but insisted on denying the existence of.

"I'm fine, really. Awesome actually." She continued to swipe her cheeks. "Now I'm going to have to fix my make-up."

"You look perfect," Peter said, adoring the way she looked when she made a fuss. "As always."

She hugged him again, this time squeezing him around the middle. "Love you," she said.

He held her close and planted a gentle kiss on the top of her head. "You'd better go. I've got to finish getting ready too. First jump is at nine."

She slipped away from him, blowing a kiss as she walked out, then turning to say, "Your fly's down." It was her classic line whenever he wore boxer shorts. He guessed she'd have a hard time erasing that smile for days. That wouldn't hurt her stage appeal, though. Peter loved watching her perform and, after their recent discussion, was more excited to see and hear her tonight.

Peter's last jump of the day had been a bit later, causing him to miss Jane's first few numbers, but she looked electrified when she saw him come in. As Jane finished her current number, Peter ordered a sandwich at the bar and took a seat at a table facing the small corner stage.

Peter paused his chewing to applaud, and Jane spoke into the microphone. "I wrote this song today after a rare and lucky strike of inspiration, and I'd like to dedicate it . . . to Peter."

Warmth flared in Peter's cheeks. He hated when she mentioned him. For a moment, he bowed his head, self-conscious about the stares that might be coming his way. Trying to forget it, he took another bite of his sandwich, the salty beef and perfect bread nearly melting away the embarrassment.

Jane picked a tune on her guitar, and as soon as the words began, Peter grew uneasy again. She'd written a few songs about Neverland, and they always unnerved him the first time he heard them. He checked over his shoulder to make sure the Tally Man wasn't there. Even though Peter knew better, that he and Jane were now safely tucked away in Ireland, with a new Irish surname, the memories frightened him. Peter's worries increased when he realized the song was not only about Neverland but about him as well. He tried to relax and just enjoy the sound of her clear voice and the picture of her sitting on that stool—legs crossed, arms hugging her guitar, and eyes closed so she could just feel the song. By now she was to the chorus.

"And you never thought you'd get away, from the fear that lived inside. And I watched you time and time again, try to push it from your mind. And even though we made mistakes, I'd do it all again. I'd come to Neverland again. To help you escape."

Enthralled, Peter focused on the words of the second verse.

"When insects glow in every shade, and the seasons never seem to change. When clouds and streams come and go, but everything else stays the same. Try to remember where you've been, but don't forget where you are now. All the lovely things you've seen are coming back to you somehow."

An instrumental bridge led into the chorus. Peter closed his eyes this time and just listened, imagining himself standing on the cliffs at the Black Caverns, looking out over Endal Ocean. No pirate ship threatened; not even a glimmer of fear could reach him. Gold and white fairies danced around him, and the perfect Summer Quarter sky enveloped him with warmth. The music slowed, and Peter thought he could feel the spray of a runaway ocean wave.

"And you never thought you'd get away, from the fear that lived inside. And I watched you time and time again, try to push it from your mind. And even though we made mistakes, I'd do it all again. I'd come to Neverland again. To help you escape."

The guitar finished, with Jane oohing along. Peter opened his eyes just in time to meet her gaze and see that smile, not the playful one, but the one that reminded him of the dimmed blue of the Never sky in Spring Quarter. The color of dawn. The color of a fairy who feels calm again after being worried. The color of reassurance.

ACKNOWLEDGMENTS

I couldn't have written this book without inspiration from the creator of the timeless character Peter Pan and his dazzling home of Neverland. Thanks, J. M. Barrie, for sparking endless imagination. I would also like to send a sincere thank you to my beta readers, Jesse Booth and Lisa Swinton. You both gave me such good feedback, and I am grateful for the gift of your time, ideas, and knowledge. A special thanks also goes to my proofers, Misty Pulsipher, Amy Johnson, and Regen Lemon. Regen Lemon also served as my creative consultant throughout the entire editing process. THANK YOU!!! I am always so grateful for my family, friends, and readers for their support and encouragement. You keep me going! Thanks also goes to the editing team at Cedar Fort. One final shout-out to my editor, Beth Bentley. You are a genius! Thank you for helping me polish my sentences and for knowing everything from basic science to advanced grammar. I don't ever want to see the word "antecedent" again, but I'm glad I now know what it means.

ABOUT THE AUTHOR

*M*elissa Lemon began twisting fairy tales in the fifth grade when she wrote a story about George of the Jungle making his way to Neverland. She has since published several novels, including *Cinder and Ella*, *Snow Whyte and the Queen of Mayhem*, and *Sleeping Beauty and the Beast*. Melissa earned a bachelor's degree from the University of Utah with a minor in creative writing. She is married to a frog prince and has spawned three princesses. She is also warden to a tolerant cat named Matilda. Melissa lives at the mouth of a windy canyon, where she is always working on her next project.

ALSO LOOK FOR

Cinder and Ella
Snow Whyte and the Queen of Mayhem
Sleeping Beauty and the Beast

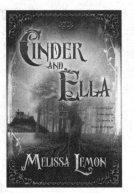

Scan to visit

www.melissalemon.com